Desert Writing
Stories from country
Edited by Terri-ann White

Desert Writing
Stories from country

Edited by Terri-ann White

UWA PUBLISHING

First published in 2016 by
UWA Publishing
Crawley, Western Australia 6009
www.uwap..com.au

UWAP is an imprint of UWA Publishing
a division of The University of Western Australia

THE UNIVERSITY OF
WESTERN
AUSTRALIA

Cover map of Paruku by the children of Mulan community with Kim Mahood.
Cover design by Greg Jorss, Upside Creative
Typeset in Bembo by J & M Typesetting
Printed by McPherson's Printing Group

This project has been assisted by the Australian Government through the Australia Council, its arts funding and advisory body.

 uwapublishing

Contents

Mulan, Western Australia

Tennant Creek, Northern Territory

Anangu Pitjantatjara Yankunytjatjara Lands, South Australia

Welcome to Desert Writing!
Terri-ann White

It may have been a visit to the Kimberley region of Western Australia that suggested it to me but then the team at UWA Publishing decided that there hadn't been enough writerly insights into the remote parts of Australia defined as 'desert' through geography and climate. Educating the coast-huggers of Australian settler populations about the contours of this vast continent and illuminating the beauty of remote places became one of our priorities. We also imagined that opportunities for people living in the desert to tell their stories and, more importantly, write them down in classes and workshops were rare.

In our pitch to the Australia Council for the Arts to make this happen with support both moral and financial we said:

> This is a unique project, one that goes beyond merely regional places; this is situated in desert areas that are so remote most will require at least ten hours drive from the nearest airport town. These are places where lives are rich, nuanced and are an integral, but often overlooked, part of our culture and identity. Often Australian states work independently on projects but this project combines two states and one territory with

professionals who are dedicated in working together
to explore the nature of deserts.

Our ambition was to enter into the three communities we'd
selected and allow both Aboriginal and non-Aboriginal people
to join a writing workshop and leave behind their writings with
us for this book. Our partners were people who knew the country: the writers' centres of South Australia and the Northern
Territory. They enabled the logistics of securing workshop leaders and people hungry to write. The participants ranged from
transient workers just arrived to generationally settled people,
and traditional owners and elders who know this country as well
as the back of their hand. At Mulan it also included the children
in all three classes at their school, the John Pujajangka-Piyirn
Catholic School.

Our initial expectations for this project and the writing
that would be our yield saw us investigating and representing
the business of isolation and extremity: the reality of Australia's
geography; the conditions of climate; the delicate dance between
original owners and custodians and the colonial past we have
inherited. Co-habitation; understanding country, the politics of
land usage, and the individual and her community are some of
the thematics and concerns we anticipated would swirl around
the approaches made in the workshops. All of these things
happened with the right tone and an individual flavour: nothing
was circumscribed by the project's intentions.

The forms of writing and the set of themes and topics of the
content are wildly diverse, as you'd expect with a large group

of people who allow their imagination to order their present, past, and future to tell stories of love and loss, everyday rituals and habits, the life of the mind and all of the struggles of being human.

After the workshops were completed and the writing started to be delivered to me in Perth, I realised what an ambitious project this really was. Some people involved were telling their stories for the first time and some were telling it for the hundredth. And how long will it take before we understand the biggest story of Australia? When will we come to a real recognition of this country: about belonging and occupation, dispossession and the wilful blindness towards our history. As well as that, to *see* this continent in all of its splendour requires, in my opinion, a visit to its desert places to observe the austere beauty and the resilience of living there where daily life contains complex knowledge and decisions we city folk can only marvel at.

The claim we made in our application to fund this anthology was that it *will be a contribution to the recognition of the desert as a significant locus in Australian culture and debate about place and belonging.* There will be both familiar and entirely novel threads through these writings for all readers, I expect, and for that we should be excited.

A note on biographical information about contributors. When required for a contextual understanding of the writer we have provided a short biography. Many of the writings include a biographical context and thus do not require further detail.

Heartfelt thanks are offered to the workshop leaders:
Marie Munkara and Ktima Heathcote
Ali Cobby Eckermann and Lionel Fogarty
Kim Mahood and Terri-ann White

Professor Julianne Schultz for advice and recommendations.
To the partners in this project:
UWA Publishing, especially Linda Martin, Charlotte Guest and student interns who assisted in transcribing tapes.

The Northern Territory Writers' Centre, particularly Panos Couros and Sally Bothroyd.

The SA Writers Centre, particularly Sarah Tooth.

The Australia Council for the Arts for their faith and enthusiasm for this project.

Cover image: a map of Paruku by the children of the Mulan community with the guidance and support of Kim Mahood.

Terri-ann White is the Director of UWA Publishing.

Kate Fielding
Warburton Tree House

From 2008 to 2011 I lived and worked in Warburton Ranges Remote Aboriginal Community, in the Ngaanyatjarra Lands, Western Australia. About 500 people live here, in the middle of an enormous desert. Space is closer (100 km above our heads) than the nearest major towns, Kalgoorlie and Alice Springs, both more than 900 km away. Warburton is the most compelling place I know.

Niketa, Talea and several other kids are sitting in the front yard when I get home from work, in a clear patch of red sand under a wattle tree. They are smoothing the sand with their small hands, back and forth, gently brushing off the top layer down to where it gets damp and will hold a line. At the same time they are rhythmically thwacking the ground with their storywires, the pieces of thick bent fence wire the kids carry bent round their necks to use as drawing tools. Thwack, thwack, thwack. They chatter and brush and thwack 'til someone has something more detailed to say. That kid's storywire will spring into action, scratching into the ground to make the lines and movement to show the idea, the story, the space between things.

'Kate, Kate, Kate, come do storywire with us!'

'Okay, just a minute, I'll put my bag down.'

'We can have a cool drink?'

'No cordial but I've got some oranges, do you want to share some?'

'Yeeeeeesss' in a chorus.

I walk inside and drop my bag on the chair, kicking off my shoes and putting on thongs as I grab the oranges from the kitchen. It delights me that kids here still have the freedom to walk around and hang out together doing their important business. It reminds me of the stories I hear from my parents, uncles and aunties of growing up in suburban Melbourne in the 1950s, when they would roam the streets and bounce in and out of each other's houses, off running through the thistles on the vacant blocks until the sun went down. To get that kind of freedom for my brothers and me my parents moved out to a farm, out in dairy country. I would go walking for hours across the farms or riding my horse, swimming in the creek with my brothers and my friends, building tiny houses out of moss for imaginary creatures or igloos woven from bushes for us all to sleep in.

Back outside, the sand has been cleared for a new story. Niketa is going to tell story. She lives two doors up from us and is both smart and naughty. For the first few weeks I thought her name was a Ngaanyatjarra swear word, because I so often heard it called out in frustration as Niketa sped past with her head down in a funny little determined run. Her house has a veranda with a wonderful view of the airstrip, and so often the older women of her family sit out there, keeping an eye on what's going on around town. I secretly call them 'the veranda ladies'; my first port of call when I need advice. Niketa motions for me to sit down in the circle, and I do, enjoying stretching my legs out on the lovely soft ground.

Niketa begins: 'We'll ask that man.' A stick figure of a man. 'Ben, with the red modabike.' Two wheels and a seat appear beside the stick figure. 'He's your kurri (husband).' A cheeky look at me. 'We'll tell him, "can we build this?"' A square, a tree beside it. 'We'll say to him: "Can we build a treehouse?"'. Thwack thwack thwack alongside the pictures of the man, the motorbike, the square and the tree. Niketa grins at me, questioning.

'That's an interesting idea. I wonder where we could build it', I say, looking around.

'Over here', they all squeal, leaping up and running across to the gumtree by the gate. Clearly this plan has been hatching over some time.

Ben and I are lying in bed on Saturday morning. Ben did some food shopping earlier in the week so we are spared the Saturday morning rush to the community's one shop to get the groceries before they close at midday, not opening again until Monday morning. Most staff shop on Saturday, which means unless you manage to squeeze it in during the week, your weekend starts with either the unrelaxing task of doing the shopping with all your workmates or forgoing fresh food.

Occasionally on the weekends we are woken by loud thumps on the roof. If the kids are wild at you they might roof rock you; lobbing fist-sized rocks which hit the metal roof with a terrifying BANG. It happened a bit when we first got here – kids testing out the new people – but it's been ages since we've been roof rocked. Instead last week I came home to find our front door had been lovingly outlined in bright pink bougainvillaea, so I walked into the house through an arch of magenta flames. The most recent roof rocking instance was not by a kid but by one of the old ladies, come to see if we might like to buy a painting at 7 a.m. on a Sunday. (No.)

But this morning all we can hear are the kids playing in the treehouse. Ben built it almost two months ago now and they've been playing there obsessively. It has two levels: a wooden floor in the fork, shadecloth surrounding that, and a metal grid top layer – good for climbing on if you are little, good for putting decorations on too. Seems like every few days we come home to find a new addition: a pan, a few clothes pegs, a rug, a garden of flowers arranged around its base. The kids are slowly making it more and more cosy. The kids are obsessively watering the tree as well, which is growing thick, luxuriant leaves in response. Grown up by fire and flood, these desert gums know how to make hay while the sun shines.

All the garden is growing. By now the front yard is cool and partially private. We've set up a couch on the front porch, and sit out there in the evenings. People drop by to visit, including the three veranda ladies: Regina, Jeanie and Roberta, three sisters who were little kids in mission times. Regina lives a few doors up from us, and her sisters often come to visit. Regina's veranda has an incredibly useful view if you are interested in the comings and goings on. You can see who is arriving at the airstrip, who is driving in on two of the major roads and across to the community office. I like that they keep an eye on our front yard.

When we arrived here Ben planted some sunflowers. They grew fast and big; flowers twice as wide as an adult's head. The veranda ladies told us that during one of our trips off the Lands they were sitting on the couch on our porch, enjoying the cool air, screened by the trees. They saw two little boys come into the garden and try to pick these sunflowers. They were trying and trying to get them down, but they couldn't. Eventually they got so frustrated they threw rocks at the flowers, and when that didn't solve it they defiantly pissed on the stem. 'Oh we were laughing, laughing, but quiet, because they didn't know we were there', the veranda ladies tell me.

One windy day I came home for lunch and found the tree had been chainsawed down.

Huh? It was right there when I left this morning! But now the tree was cut down to the floor of the bottom level, and the branches all dragged into a pile. What the hell happened?

I went inside in a daze, got my apple and then walked over to the veranda ladies, rolling my hand in the hand sign for question.

'Yuwa (yes), that man been come and chop it down, it was fire at the top.'

'Wiya (no), not fire, them things, sparks, there was sparking up top.'

'Yuwa yuwa yuwa, sparks, that tree was rubbing them wires, making sparks!'

This made sense, there'd been fierce wind all day. Tropical cyclone Laurence, a category five cyclone which had been tracking down the WA coast for days, was finally headed inland straight for us. During the beginning of these cyclone winds the top of the tree was rubbing the electrical lines, and started sparking, a huge cascade of sparks.

Someone jumped in and chainsawed the tree down, stopping the sparks but destroying the treehouse.

This morning when I was driving to work the veranda ladies called me over. 'They shouldn't have cut that tree right down, they should have just trimmed it.' Regina was fired up, grumpy. Jeanie was morose, like she'd seen it all before. Roberta, with her immaculate white bob, was getting on with some carving.

'Look, we got that wood, we making punu (small carved wooden things)!'

'Yuwa, that makes me pukurlpa (happy)', I said. 'It's not getting wasted, it's getting used. I was feeling sad for that tree and that treehouse. But I'm glad you are making something with it.'

'Yuwa', they all laughed, 'ninti-one-pa (clever one)!'

Roberta carved away on a skinny bit of wood, joking about how all the tjinka (sand goannas) are getting skinny.

A few weeks later I go and get some punu for my brothers for Christmas, made from that tree that got cut down. Some days life here seems impossibly harsh, and then something like this reminds you all over again that these things go around and around and around and all you can do is enjoy the upswings.

We get home from Christmas leave and the tree is already growing back. On Saturday at sunset, there's storms all around: the sky is full of electric thunder. I dreamt last night that Warburton was in a ring of fire. It's been 45 degrees Celsius for most of the day.

Dust storms are turning the sky to pink and orange in all directions, and the sunset is golden. Ben and I go to sit out by the regrowing tree to watch the lightning coming closer. There are forks cracking across the Ranges – first above them and then inside, coming across the plain toward us. A double rainbow erupts amongst it all, and curtains of rain are hanging off the clouds, evaporating before they hit the hot hot ground. We can see two dust storms rolling in from different directions, the Ranges disappearing behind them and trees slowly disappearing too as they get closer and closer. A senior Ngaanyatjarra couple, Ruby and Burt, drive past in a ute, excited, hanging out the window, slowing down to wave excitedly at us. Cars are circling around town, looking for the best view.

We race inside when the really big wind front comes through in case there's loose sheet iron around, and then race out to my car once it has passed. Jump in, the lightning is cracking down well this side of the ranges now and we drive over to pick up our friends JB and Alex, and then out to the sandhill in the rain to try and get a good view. We drive up the top, the rain's passed and we lie down watching stars and lightning crack above us. Each time it cracks we 'oh' and 'wow' like fireworks. JB is frantically setting up a camera. The lightning is a warm yellow, apricot, thick bars of it. We see an orange glow on the horizon; it gets redder and redder and the sun is gone down past the horizon until we are sure it is a fire.

The storms are passing over, we shake the sand off our backs and out of our pants, jump in the car again, and drive out to the Telstra tower, up to the hill to try to get an eyeline to the fire. Cam and Silvana and Archie the dog catch up with us in Cam's troopie. It glows brighter and brighter, but still no flames in view, just the glow reflected off smoke. The first fire dies down without flames, but another picks up and we all climb on top of the cars trying to see, and can just see flames at either edge. We can see four other fires as well, a couple more starting whilst we are watching. Lightning storms in all directions.

We lie down in a circle in the middle of the road, looking up at the stars which are clear above us, but ringed by storm. Cam hugging Archie the dog. All the other things we were going to do forgotten. So much space around us, such long views, this incredible electric night.

By next August the tree is big enough that the treehouse is being built again. One Saturday night we drag the telly outside and put it up on the treehouse platform to watch the federal election. We light an enormous bonfire to keep us warm and put our swags out on the ground. The election goes late into the night, and we watch and wait with that blazing fire, for a result that doesn't arrive. Cars swing by slowly, cruising around town. Niketa and her mates stop by on their way home from some adventure. The veranda ladies come across to see the fire. We drink tea. The stars swing above us, the Milky Way shimmers and it is closer to outer space than anywhere else. The big open sky seems just wide enough to hold all this richness, this complexity, this love.

The desert stretches around us forever, in all directions, for all time.

Kate Fielding builds creative platforms for intercultural conversations. She is a cultural strategist, a writer of narrative non-fiction and an advocate for social change hairdressing. Kate is a 2014-2016 Sidney Myer Creative Fellow. She is currently writing a book about how hairdressing can change the world.

Holly Ringland
Lost Girl of the Never-Never

*But we who have lived in it, and loved it, and left it, know
that our hearts can Never-Never rest away from it.*

— JEANNIE GUNN

The morning dawns in Manchester and I am woken by the
purple light. I slip from the feathery warmth of bed and pad
downstairs in the same ugg boots I've had since I was twenty-
three. Red dirt still stains their soles. I make coffee and scuff
back upstairs, inhaling my steaming brew. I open the door to
my office, close it behind me, and turn a lamp on. Muted light
pools on my writing desk. Icicles clinging to the window are
unaffected by the sunrise; it looks fiery, but holds no heat. I
place my coffee on my desk and fill the bowl of my oil burner
with water. I add a few drops of Australian eucalyptus oil and
light a candle, which I slide into the belly of the burner. Three
seed pods sitting on a small dish nearby are illuminated in the
candlelight. I pick one up and press it into my palm as I flick
through my notebook to get to a fresh, clean page. The sharp
edges of the seed pod leave red indents in my skin. I unscrew
the cap of my fountain pen. The candlewick hisses as it burns.

I close my eyes and hear the pop and hiss of the fire in my yard, reaching for the glitter of unfettered desert stars. The red dirt is warm beneath my bare feet. The flowering gums and thryptomene fill the summer night air with a heady sweetness. I open my eyes, back at my desk in England. Outside leafless silver birches sway in the cold, milky light. I put the seed pod back on the dish with the others and grip my pen in earnest as I start writing on the new page. This is my morning ritual. I do this every day to conjure the Western Desert landscape and bring it back to me, here, a decade and half the world away.

When I was twenty-three years old I moved from the Gold Coast to Yulara, the resort township twenty-five kilometres from Uluru in the Northern Territory. Raised barefoot on the southeast Queensland coast, living anywhere too far from water had never appealed to me. After returning home from a post-university escape to Canada, I plunged back into the familiarity of Gold Coast life and found my contempt breeding at every corner. Hungry to flee, I was seeking escape again when a friend got hospitality work at Yulara, in the Northern Territory. It sounded like a completely different life to the one I knew by the sea. There were more jobs available, which came with housing – all I had to do was get myself there. Having never been to the Northern Territory before, I only had the mythology of *Crocodile Dundee* and Dick Roughsey's books from my childhood to inform my adult imagination. As I packed my bag the very last thing I was expecting was that I would develop a relationship with the Western Desert that would alter my life irrevocably.

I flew into Connellan Airport at Uluru from Brisbane and spent the flight sitting transfixed by the window, watching the Earth slowly turn from green to brown, to the fiery Outback red I had long heard of but never seen firsthand. Uluru rose from the vast, flat land surrounding it like an elaborately carved dream. The grandeur of it would never fail to astonish me. From the air the resort township of Yulara looked like an urban peapod growing obstinately from the desert with its hotel sails, swimming pools, and manicured grass. I was more interested in how green the surrounding native landscape was. Gullies of desert oaks and occasional gums rippled along sand dunes, skirted by mulga shrubs and rounds of spinifex. I twitched with the nervous thrill of a new beginning.

My plane landed. As I disembarked the air hit me like a gust coming out of a hot oven. It was light and dry, not heavy and humid like the coastal climate I'd left behind. The searing heat was unlike anything I had ever known. It left me short of breath and thirstier than I could recall being. I squinted in the glare of the day. The colours were so vibrant my eyes watered. My sensory register was saturated with the strangeness of the red dirt, blue sky, and green flora of the desert.

The peapod was a cranking, bustling tourist machine. I was collected by the resort's human relations team and crammed into a staff flat that was built for two but was used by the resort to house four. My flatmates were kind, and I was grateful. Orientation began the next day. I expected a hike, or an immersion in the desert-scape. We were instead put in a fluorescently lit room to learn about cultural awareness and resort code of conduct from printed leaflets.

During my first week in the desert it rained. I ran out of my flat into it in disbelief, after only having been away from water for a few days. The smell of it hitting the red dirt was so evocative, I still pine for the scent. It was all of the best things, but even better. Freshly brewed coffee, moss, baked bread, the ocean, a new fire. It was for me even better to smell the rain in the desert than it was to see it. The next morning wildflowers had popped up overnight from the earth. I was bewildered by such natural magic.

I very quickly learned privacy was the most coveted commodity in resort staff housing. I found mine on long walks in the afternoon amongst the undulating sand dunes surrounding the resort. I often sat in a silent stupor on the soft, red sand to watch the dramatic colours of sunset change the sky. When I started my job at the hotel I often took an hour to walk a kilometre to work, stopping to notice a honey grevillea bud, or a huddle of Sturt's desert peas in bloom. Finding a thorny devil crossing my path gave me enough joy to see me through my oncoming shift. The vastness of the desert brought me great comfort. The strangeness of the red landscape filled the emptiness inside me. I was insatiable for it and wanted somehow to envelop it, this otherworld, as if I might be able to breathe it in to the veins beneath my skin.

In contrast to my sensory engagement with the desert, I struggled with the brutality of my experience working for the resort. Blatant bigotry, racism, and sexism thrived at the executive level and quickly embittered my new world. When I heard that Uluru-Kata Tjuta National Park was looking for someone with a communications degree to work in their media compliance office, I leapt at the chance. The malaise of the resort's microcosm culture and its disconnection from the surrounding living landscape and its people was unbearable; I wanted nothing to do with the former. My feelings were cemented when I resigned. After I explained to the hotel that I'd been offered a job using my communications degree to work at federal government level for the national park, the general manager leant back in his chair and hooked his thumbs through the d-loops of his belt. *They're a wild bunch of cowboy hooligans out there*, he snorted in the back of his throat, sneering at me. *You'll probably get raped. Good luck.* Needless to say, my resignation notice turned into quitting on the spot.

My job with the national park involved assessing media permit requests to ensure they complied with protecting the cultural values of the land, one of the strongest being its stories. However, despite my degree and past work experience, I was only competent in my position once I had learned the stories embedded in the landscape – the two are interchangeable, as real as each other. In order to protect sacred sites from being captured or used by media for commercial purposes, I had to first understand and memorise the land, where the sites were around Uluru and Kata Tjuta, and why they were sacred, and then learn the living stories significant to each site. Essentially it was my responsibility to learn and uphold the values of a culture totally foreign to me, yet fundamentally Australian. Through Anangu stories and law the desert came to figurative and literal life right before my eyes. I had stumbled into an Australia I had never known – neither in my schooling nor in my upbringing. An elderly man told me that any Australian at any point in time has more than 60,000 years of stories at their fingertips – all we have to do is ask. I asked whenever I could, consumed and fascinated by the transformation of what I thought I knew about what it meant to me to be an Australian. Every day was challenging, hard, meaningful, and substantial. I loved it.

The first time in my life I lived alone was in a two-bedroom semi-detached besser block house on the outskirts of Rangerville, the arm of park staff housing in Mutitjulu. I had a large yard full of thryptomene and spinifex, framed by desert oaks, in the centre of which was a fire pit encircled by logs. I lit fires even in the middle of summer. I strung fairy lights around the frame of the back patio and tied a hammock between two of the posts, which I lay in to get full sun on winter mornings while I read a book. Inside I filled the house with pot plants I bought on air-conditioned road trips to Kmart in Alice Springs, and art and craft from the Pitjantjatjara lands, imbued with local stories. I set up a writing desk that faced the large glass back doors, with an outlook into my red, green, blue, and golden garden. My need to escape evaporated. I let my feet touch the ground.

After my first couple of years living and working in the park I noticed that although I loved my job there was still a level of disconnection from country. Although my work was Uluru-centric, I was removed from engaging with the landscape the way I most desired. My general working week was spent managing the paperwork of media requests, assessing images of Uluru, and supervising film crews capturing images of the park from ground or air to ensure they complied with Commonwealth Reserve legislation – while Uluru stood right outside my office window (which was known amongst park staff as The Fishbowl). Away from Visitor Services, on the Operations side of the park, I was occasionally called upon to scale Uluru as part of the park's Vertical Rescue team, which rescued tourists who had openly ignored the requests not to climb and the warning signs about personal safety. I had never climbed Uluru recreationally. The distance and disparity from the land I felt in my job was at times jarring. Sometimes I would get home from work, draw the curtains, have a hot shower, and not want to see a speck of red dirt. Those nights left me out of sorts. Whenever I got the chance to step away from the metaphorical lights of the tourist circus, I sought solace from connecting to country through its stories, both the ones I had learned from others, and the ones that were my own.

When I was twenty-six I fell in love at Kuniya Piti, a sacred site at the northeast corner of Uluru where Kuniya, the Python Woman, carefully placed her eggs before going into a raging battle at Mutitjulu Waterhole. Drawn there at the same time each day by our coinciding schedules, we would 'accidentally' meet just before sunset and sit at Kuniya Piti for a while together. Through conversation we carefully revealed parts of ourselves to each other, while yellow butterflies fluttered around us in the orange air, drunk on the flame-light of the setting sun.

Later the next year the desert landscape was the catalyst that brought my estranged father back into my life. He drove three thousand kilometres from the Gold Coast into the Western Desert to meet me. The last time he had seen me I was a teenager. Very few of my colleagues understood why I went pale after the Entry Station staff had rung me to let me know my dad had just passed through the gate and was on his way out to meet me at The Fishbowl. I walked out to the car park to meet him. I waited with Uluru behind me, surrounded by clustered desert oaks, taking comfort in my ranger uniform, in the sturdiness of my boots.

Although I worked in a land of wide open spaces, what I craved most at the end of each work day in the desert was space. Most afternoons when I walked through my front door I was already half out of my uniform. Straight into 'civvies', running shoes on. I took my camera, notebook and pen, and wandered the eight-kilometre track that looped behind my house. Sometimes I didn't stop, except to try and photograph the sunset softening Uluru's stature. When I did pause, it was most often to stand idle between two desert oaks, tall and grandmotherly in character. Leant against their bases I sat and used my knees as a desk to write. One afternoon on the way home I found a broken music box on the track. I opened the lid and tried to wind it, without success. I have never stopped wondering what tune it might have played.

My relationship with the desert isn't just marked by prominent cultural or personal stories. Some of the most meaningful experiences I recall are when nothing much happened. I'd sit on one of the cut gum logs in the circle around the fire pit in my back yard and watch the desert oak silhouettes sway in early starlight. The scent of baked earth intermingled with the fire smoke. The pale blooms of thryptomene and wild desert roses in the yard surrounding me dotted the violet smudge of dusk. Laughter and squeals coming from kids playing in the community wafted over the sand dunes with the cacophony of community dogs barking as the sun went down. In that time between day and night when the earth settled, there was a pulse to things. It beat in my wrists. The moon climbed into the flawless inky sky. The wind sighed. I would let my fire burn down, and go inside to fall asleep to the last sounds of it crackling to embers.

The four years I spent in the desert enriched, shattered, and transformed my life. My experience working for Uluru-Kata Tjuta National Park and living in Mutitjulu Community later included the overwhelming reality of the Northern Territory Intervention – controversial, widely criticised changes to welfare provision, law enforcement, land tenure and other measures introduced by the Australian federal government under John Howard in 2007 to address allegations of child sexual abuse and neglect in Northern Territory Aboriginal communities – and what quickly became a mentally, emotionally, and physically violent relationship with the love I'd found at Kuniya Piti. I kept the latter hidden, until I finally acknowledged I was at risk, emotionally and geographically isolated with this volatile secret. I left on a Sunday morning without farewell, or resolution. I was at work on Friday as usual, but by Monday I had vanished. With the help of a few colleagues I had fled, after it had become clear that such an action was the only one to take. My life in the desert was severed. That was 2008. It has taken the seven years since for me to learn how to separate the psychological landscape of traumatic experience from the physical desert landscape, and in that process draw an understanding of why and how the Western Desert meant so much to my life, and still does.

There were two main things I remember learning when I first arrived in Yulara. One was the general consensus amongst resort staff that whitefellas only ended up there if they were running from the law, or themselves. I was no criminal, but I also was no exception to that rule.

The other I came across in the introduction to a copy of *Peter Pan* I'd unwittingly packed and taken to the desert with me. In the earliest drafts of JM Barrie's play, he had called the island 'Peter's Never-Never Land', possibly inspired by 'the Never-Never', the name given to the Australian Outback by Barcroft Boake in his poem *Where the Dead Men Lie*. This idea had a profound effect on me. As I found my way in the desert from job to job and housing to housing, I thought about never-places and how being immersed in them was a contradic-tory constant. Just like the Lost Boys had found a home amidst the beautiful, brutal landscape of Never-Land, my escape to the Western Desert had given my life a similar sense of meaning. Through immersing myself in the culture, language and stories of the desert, listening to and learning from people so willing to share, my identity as an Australian and a global citizen was dimensioned and transformed. Far from being a Never-Never, the Western Desert is a place where the past and present live side by side. It is where I gained an experiential understanding of how everything can be connected to something else, through nature, story, memory, and song – through a timelessness that doesn't exist in urban landscapes. Unlike in Boake's poem, the desert to me is no dead, never-place. It is teeming and pulsing with thrumming, vital, living culture.

This morning at my desk, I added Australian sandalwood to my usual eucalyptus oil blend. The warm and spicy scent reminds me a bit of the smell of mulga wood. Outside the window of my office I can see Manchester's red brickscape glisten in the wet morning. I chose this room in my house to write in because of its outlook. At certain times of day the red brick is illuminated by sunlight and blazes fiery, like the sun's last rays gilding the western face of Uluru. My daily routine can sometimes change. Maybe tomorrow morning, for instance, I'll listen to the CD I played most in my work truck and there I'll be in my ranger boots, working the pedals and gears of the troopie, wiping the sweat from my top lip in the desert heat. The seed pods are ever-present on my desk. They were given to me by an old desert friend to remind me that some things need fire to split open and grow. I recall what a filmmaker I worked with at the national park said to me once. *This is your fuel, you know. One day it will catch fire.* I had vehemently shaken my head. *Nah. I won't ever write about this place. I don't have the room. It's too big.* Which was true. I didn't have room. And, yet, ten years later here I am, conjuring the desert through the process of writing my first novel.

Until I sat down to write this article I wasn't fully aware of the daily motions I go through at my desk. I've considered why I practise these rituals and they are a process akin to taking your shoes off before you enter a temple; these are my preparations and prayers before I immerse myself in a space that is sacred. However, even deeper than that is my knowledge of how the desert is a living landscape: I don't actually need a ritual or a daily practice to visit it. The Western Desert will never be any further from me than the second between my heart's beats, or the un-seeable dark in the blink of my eye. The desert is always there. Here. It has gone through me, and soaked my life with its colour. I have lived in it, loved it, and left it. Perhaps the simplest truth is that my heart will never, never rest away from it.

Holly Ringland is an Australian writer and advocate of stories for change. lived in a camper van on the road in the US for two years, which inspired a lifelong interest in cultures, landscapes, and stories. In 2011 Holly gained her MA in Creative Writing from the University of Manchester, and has been living between England and Australia since. The dissertation Holly wrote that explores the four years of her twenties she spent living in Australia's western desert. In 2015 the first chapter of Holly's forthcoming debut novel won Griffith Review's annual writing award. She is currently in the final year of her Creative Writing PhD with Griffith University and King's College London. Both Holly's forthcoming novel and academic research explore domestic violence by taking an introspective look at how positive meaning can be drawn from traumatic experience through the creative writing process; how unspoken past trauma can be conjured and spoken, transformed, or reformed, through writing fiction. www.hollyringland.com

Mulan,
Western Australia

Kim Mahood
Introduction:
Writing from the desert – Paruku

The Australian desert is a more complicated place than it used to be. There was a time when it functioned in the white Australian imagination more as a metaphor than a real place, a negative space into which explorers, white children and the occasional eccentric wanderer disappeared, leaving a frisson of existential anxiety and a satisfying conviction that the heart of the continent remained an impenetrable mystery. Its nomadic occupants, for the most part invisible, were stone age remnants – innocent, bloodthirsty, fabulous and doomed.

Until the last decades of the twentieth century most of the words written about the desert and its occupants were written by white people – journalists, historians, anthropologists, novelists, settler wives – with varying degrees of insight, curiosity, incomprehension and mythologising.

This solipsistic condition started to unravel with the emergence of the Western Desert painting movement in the 1970s and 1980s, which has in recent times effloresced into a cultural renaissance of astonishing vigour and originality. The iconic desert nomads, instead of fading discreetly into the mirage along with their obscure traditions, emerged in the vanguard of contemporary culture as charismatic individuals with rich and entertaining personal histories, as well as disturbing tales of displacement and murder. It turned out that they weren't even proper nomads, but the custodians of clearly defined tracts of land, the boundaries of which they transgressed at their peril. The desert, or deserts, for there are many different deserts in Australia, each of them with their own particular character, began to speak through the voices of the people who called them home.

The stories were encoded in the paintings, epics in which individual lives intersected with ancestral creation stories, and the beginnings of an understanding of the complexity of Aboriginal belief systems began to infiltrate the broader Australian culture. As the painting movement expanded, a more literal story-telling element emerged – of the frontier contact days, of growing up on the missions and cattle stations, of making the adaptations and adjustments necessary to the changes in their world.

Recognising that the desert is rich with stories of real people and particular places has not displaced the metaphoric space it occupies in our cultural imagination, but it has destabilised it, opened it up to challenge and re-interpretation. Painting, sculpture, dance, and oral histories have all gone a long way towards weaving strands of brilliant colour through a once monochrome fabric.

But that most subtle and individual form of narrative expression, writing, is still not much practised as a means of telling desert stories.

When Terri-ann White contacted me about co-ordinating a writing workshop in the remote Aboriginal community of Mulan, where I work for several months each year, I assumed she meant the sort of event to which people fly or drive at great expense, in order to experience the glamour of the desert along with the stimulus of a professional workshop. The part of the desert where I work is not associated with writing as literature. Those of the population who have competent literacy skills are more likely to be called on to translate the mysteries of a Centrelink form than to be invited to write the story of a personal experience.

So I was intrigued when the model Terri-ann revealed was to draw on writing from the place itself. I wondered how to do so when much of the population was not literate, and those who were did not associate literacy with story-telling. It would be necessary to stretch the definition of 'writing' to include the oral traditions of the desert people, and to allow for a spectrum of story-telling models. I told Terri-ann I'd do my best, but I couldn't guarantee the outcomes. Having facilitated various workshops and meetings over the past decade, I wasn't about to make promises I couldn't keep.

On the other hand I had learned to trust serendipity, especially around projects that involved storytelling and country. These are things Aboriginal people care about. We could involve the schoolkids, through the language and literacy program. The older people were always happy to tell their stories, various configurations of the dance between the mission, the station and the bush. There were a few *kartiya* (white people) who would be happy to participate, and I could probably persuade some of the Balgo mob to come over for a day of storytelling.

We spent a day in the school, adapting a model to suit the senior kids, the middle school and the little ones. They were full of enthusiasm, the paramount story being a hunting adventure on the weekend in which a dog brought down a kangaroo. Some wrote their own stories, while others dictated to the teachers, who honoured the poetics of the Aboriginal English spoken by the children. This was an excursion into literature, not grammar, and it was the authenticity of the kids' voices that needed to be on the page. In particular there was the story of Junior Ovi, lost in Melbourne on a school excursion, using his desert-honed skills of observation to find his way back to the hotel.

Another day was dedicated to local adults, who told stories I knew from many tellings. It reminded me of my own childhood, listening to the adults around me tell their signature stories over and over, laying in a template of storytelling to which I am still addicted, of listening to people construct the scaffolding of events that constitute their lives.

My friend Samantha Togni was visiting the nearby community of Balgo, and I prevailed on her to bring some of the Balgo mob over for a writing session. Sam arrived with a loaded troop carrier, a dozen people including three white women who were working or volunteering in the art centre and the women's cultural centre. The group represented a spectrum of literacy one could not have assembled by design, from a Queensland university undergraduate studying contemporary literature to an elderly Kukatja artist lifted by helicopter from the desert as a malnourished child.

The workshop shaped itself around storytellers and scribes. Those who could write transcribed for those who could not. There was a clear commitment to the process, affirming that to be heard, to have one's own experience acknowledged, recorded and validated, seems to be one of the imperatives of our time.

There was a difference between the white writers and the

black, of course. For the whitefellas the experience was, and always is, about the attempt to make sense of where they are, to interpret the complexities of the place they have chosen for one reason or another to visit and live in. The Aboriginal stories are testimonial – this is my place, this is my genealogy, this is who I am. Or they are existential – a desert childhood disrupted by a helicopter flight, a sudden excision from one reality into another that equates to an abduction by aliens (a life-saving abduction in this particular case) – the stretch between traditional life in the desert and life in the Mission dormitories under a regime of God and cleanliness and obedience.

This hybrid ground, where two sensibilities encountered each other, in which meanings were misinterpreted, lost, wilfully misunderstood, and yet have endured in ways that make them impossible to ignore or forget, underlies the fluid contemporary culture of the desert.

The value of a book like this is that it celebrates this hybrid existence, revealing our shared human need to tell our stories, regardless of race and culture – and our differences, that each person's world can be barely comprehensible to another.

This section of the book will be a challenge to the reader expecting a conventional series of stories about life in the desert. To mediate between the written word, designed for publication, and the performed word, designed to captivate an audience in a particular moment, requires a flexible relationship with what constitutes writing. Much of what is written here should be approached as a form of poetry, to be heard as much as read. To appreciate the rhythms and cadences of Aboriginal English, to recognise the style of individual voices, I would suggest to the reader that if something in a story eludes you, read it aloud so you can hear the patterns of the voice, and listen for whatever comes through.

I am looking forward to taking the book back to Mulan, in particular to the school, showing the children their own words in print, having them read those words aloud to their teachers and families. It is my hope that one or more among them will understand the power of the written word as a story-telling tool, will some day transform literacy into literature and go on to tell their stories in a language that carries all the nuances and subtleties of their rich and complex place.

Kim Mahood is a writer and artist based in Wamboin near Canberra. She grew up in Central Australia and on Tanami Downs Station, and has maintained strong connections with the Warlpiri traditional owners of the station and with the families of the Walmajarri stockmen who worked with her family. She is the author of *Craft for a Dry Lake*, which won several awards for non-fiction including the Age Book of the Year and the NSW Premier's Award. Her essays have been published in art, literary and public affairs journals, and her artwork is held in state, territory and regional collections. She co-edited the book *Desert Lake: art, science and stories from Paruku*, published by CSIRO in 2013.

For the past nine years Kim has worked with the Walmajarri people of Paruku (Lake Gregory) on cultural and environmental mapping projects, and has facilitated and participated in art, science, writing, film and radio projects with the Walmajarri. Her new book *Position Doubtful: mapping landscapes and memories* will be published in 2016 by Scribe.

Helicopter Tjungurrayi

I been stop in desert in Ngangangara soakwater. That's the first time I been see 'em helicopter. Helicopter been bring biscuit, sugar, and weeties and flour and tealeaf. He been give'm to every camp, came down from the sky. We been tell 'em you mob go to Natawalu Well made by kartiya on the Canning Stock Route.

We been go there walking to Natawalu. I been stop there now. I been come to Balgo then because I was sick one. I been talk Wangkajungka and Mandiltjarra but no English. The people been go hunting now, I been go behind in the helicopter. Helicopter brought me to Kanningarra, I been stop there. Then right up to Kururungku. After that I went to Balgo because no medicine in Kururungku. I been take off again to Balgo. After there I been stop in old Balgo. They been load me in a big truck and I been go right up to Halls Creek. From there I been go Derby in a plane. I bin stop there till I'm strong one, I been to Balgo then.

When I was perishing, I was praying, and then I been found water.

All my people still in the desert. Jupiter Well is my father's country. Till then I been stop Balgo, I been work cutting timber – desert oak for fence post. I been help build windmill and tank at Len's Bore and Yunpu. I help with drilling bore at Durbai and Kilingkarra because water ran out at Old Mission.

Helicopter Tjungarayi is well recognised as one of Warlayirti Artists' leading artists and is a great ambassador for the Art Centre. Born at Nynmi, west of Kiwirrkurra, Helicopter learnt from a young age the location of water sources and how to hunt for bush food. When he was a young boy he became very sick and was brought into old Balgo mission in a helicopter that had been doing mining exploration work in the area. This was the first helicopter many of the people had seen and it is how he got his name. Helicopter is a Maparn (traditional healer) and is an active Law man.

Wuntupayi Jane Gimme

My mother[1] was born at Nyilla. When she was one year old, my grandmother, her mother, died and my grandfather went away with another wife. He left the kids and my mother's three big sisters looked after her. Then they moved to Kunawarritji. When she was six years old she was married to her promised husband. Her sisters told her, 'You have to stay with him, so he can look after you'. All her big sisters went away, you know. One of her sisters was hunting around in a sacred ground and they speared her and she died.

Then my mother moved south with her husband. She had three girls. When old man and mum were getting water ready for hunting, they saw some bullock coming out of the bushes. Mum was so frightened. Dad said, 'Go and hide the girls in the bushes because mamu (devils) are coming to eat us!' So she took the three girls into the bushes and she dug a hole for her and the girls to hide in. Then my father started spearing the bullock.

And they was walking around and there was no feed you know, no goannas. 'Why can't we follow those drovers?' Then one of the stockmen told them to follow them and they headed

---

1   Jane's mother was Eubena Nampitjin, who became a highly acclaimed artist working through Warlayirti Artists in Balgo.

north along the stock route. The drovers gave them clothes but my father told them not to wear the clothes, you know, because they might get stuck in their skin. They dug a hole in the sand and buried the clothes because they were frightened of them. Oh yarwyi!

When they were halfway they met Helicopter's family and my father told them, 'We are going that way', you know, north, following the drovers to the lake.

So they followed them and then when they came to the lake they were so frightened of that big water. They were frightened because they had never seen a big water before, only smaller rock holes and soak waters in their country.

They went to the old station and my mother was washing clothes for them. One Aboriginal stockman told them, 'You got to go to Balgo, there's plenty of mungarri (food) there'. And so they went to Balgo. Father Alphonse asked my mother, 'Is there any people still in the bush?' She told him, 'Yes, there's plenty there at Ngatawali'. Sister (nun) took my three sisters to the dormitory. The sisters taught them how to cook and wash clothes.

Then I was born in Old Mission. When I was five years old I went into the dormitory and my sisters looked after me. When I was in the dormitory, I used to run back to the camp to my mum and she used to take me back to dormitory. When I was older, six or seven, I used to stay there at the dormitory, I didn't run away then.

We moved to new Balgo.

When I was a little girl in the dormitory, one night we were sleeping, my mother came and peeped through the window and told us there some wunya puntu (featherfoot) around. She really made us frightened you know. So we all started to sleep tight together.

One day sister bought us a bike to ride around, you know. First she gave it to Dulcie so she can try it. She tried to ride it but she fell down: 'I don't know how to ride it'. Then she gave it to Joanne and she fell down too. Then me the same, we all fell down. Then Sister told us that you've got to pedal right 'round. Then Dulcie was going too fast and she was bumping all the girls. She was trying to put the brakes on but couldn't!

One day when I was sitting in the playground, I saw mum and dad coming, you know, and they had a little damper for me. My father was hiding all the goannas behind his back so I couldn't see. He told me, 'Nothing, no goanna' but I could see the tail! He said he's got nothing and I said, 'What's this behind you?' and he laughed. I shared the goanna with Dulcie and Joanna.

We went back to Well 33 to visit my mother's country in 2005. My mother came and Helicopter, Tjumpo, Nyumi, Eva and Mena and that old man Tjungurrayi. We went and picked up Nganyapa and she and mum took us first to Witji where the Kinyu[2] holes are. We stayed there for a little while and Nganyapa and mum talked to Kinyu. Then we went to the rockhole Muntagayi; this was where mum and her family used to go and get all the water. She told us this is where they used to sleep under that tree near the waterhole. Then we went back to the camp at 33. That night Kinyu came to visit us. My mother saw that little hopping mouse and it was Kinyu. He was hopping round near my mother. She was very, very happy to see Kinyu.

---

2   Kinyu is a spirit dog that takes care of Jane's mother's family and all the water-holes in their country around Kunawarritji (Well 33). Kinyu can take many different forms to show him/herself.

That night Kinyu was licking around my mother's neck to make her be strong. In the early morning we heard Kinyu howling letting us know that he's going back to his home.

Monica and Kim Mahood

KM: Monica, you were telling me how PayiPayi nearly killed you. How come PayiPayi nearly killed you? Was she going to kill you because it wasn't your country?

M: 'It's not your country, it's my country', she said. PayiPayi.

KM: So, what then? She try to kill you? What with? Spear?

M: Nothing. I was growling her.

KM: Monica, what's your home country?

M: Munandagallup.

KM: You're not going back? Why aren't you going back?

M: Jealous people! Do you know PayiPayi?

KM: I do know PayiPayi.
What did you do in the dormitory and growing up?

M: Going away to chasing all the stockmen!

KM: White ones or black ones?

M: White ones!

KM: So what happened? You run away, chasing those jackaroos?

M: Run away. Three girls.

KM: Did you catch those jackeroos?

M: Giving us, one by one, blanket. Sleeping in the middle.

KM: What happened when you grew up in Balgo?

M: Boarding. Garden. Cutting wood.

KM: Cutting wood for burning or for building?

M: Burning wood! For bakery.

KM: Did you work in the bakery?

M: Garden.

KM: Where was your sister then?

M: She was working. Droving.

KM: When did you find your husband?

M: We were running away from Father McGuire. Scared of mother-in-law, and running away from Father. My sister said, 'You've got to go back'.

KM: So you still didn't tell us how you found your husband. Where did you find him? One of those stockman?

M: Yeah, stockman.

KM: And you went to school in Balgo?

M: Sometimes run away. Yeah. I was hiding. Three girls run away.

KM: Where were they running away from?

M: From the mission.

KM: To meet boys or because they didn't like it?

M: They were getting beltings. The other three run off to chase the young stockmen.

They used to get hiding because they used to run away from their mission duties and all that. But needed like, boyfriend, you know.

So they took off, chasing those stockmen, but Father McGuire got them back and gave them a hiding.

Gracie Mosquito

My father Kimiti is the owner of the lake. My father had ten children of his own and he had five wives and last of all my father had my young mother; her name was Daisy Yoomarie. And my father used to live around the lake with all his other children: Harry Chungulla, George Wallaby, Biddy Chungulla, Violet Campbell, Ivan Holliman, Jimmy Smith, Nora Mundijerry, Roger Burgu and I am the youngest of all, Gracie Mosquito. My father's brother was Toby Wangke. When I come out to the lake it makes me feel good of my ancestors, just like they are walking with me here at the lake. My father's camp was the two trees called Kiji. My father used to live around here with all my elder brothers and sisters.

My father used to make a hollow log to catch fish. He used to block the one side of the log with the mud.

Desert make me feel good in my heart.

In the early days out at the old Balgo mission I used to stay in the dormitory with the rest of the girls there. While I was there I used to miss my family. I was alright staying there, but one morning some of the girls wake me up. They told me to come along with them. I was wondering because I was a new girl bought into the dormitory, so I followed them along down to the goat yard to see what's going to happen. They started milking the goats in the little tins. When we're finished we all run down the creek and start making fire to cook the milk. We all drink the milk and came back to the dormitory looking innocent. The old women go down to the goat yard to milk the goats, but could not get any milk, so Father McGuire was wild with all the women.

Joan Marie Nagomara

In the early thirties those people came. They were teenagers too. Young girls came with their father and mother. They had no napalu (boobs). With their father, mother, aunts, uncles, grandfather, grandmother. They all live in the desert, those Kukatja People.

Dennis Camp was their ceremony place, Kiwirrkurra was their country.

Father came from Broome with his donkeys. He told them, 'I'm going to the desert'. He told the police and they told him, 'You can't go, you'll die'.

'If you go out there to desert there's no people out there', his father told him. But he packed his donkey anyway and he went and he found the people.

'I'm still going, there's people out there, I know, the Lord told me.'

He used to grab them and put clothes on them!

They all came from different tribes, Kukatja, Ngardi, Ngalia. Some of our family they went to Billiluna – some went east and our family came north, they were all separate but came to live in one group. His grandfather told him, 'Go bring those people, there's water here'.

The other brother was Frank. They started to move out after that – to Comet near Mulan, and they stayed there until the forties, then in the fifties they moved to Balgo. And they all stayed.

My father was working there. He used to help them bring supplies back on the conmer (truck).

A big truck came into Gordon Downs picking up young men and putting them on truck to take to Alice Springs. When they stopped in Tanami for a break he ran away, he ran to the desert. He found his father-in-law. They were all crying asking him, 'How did you get away?', and they took him back to Balgo. Before they went to Balgo, they went to Billiluna. He met one pretty lady there – Mungka – and that was his wife. He brought her back to Balgo. She had a seven-year-old daughter and they went and found a big lake.

My little sister, she found this tin and she was filling it up with bush onions. The other kids all stole the tin and she cried and cried until they gave the tin back.

In the fifties my father found my mother, Rita Nampitjin. He had two wives. His first wife had five kids and his second wife had seven.

My dad went back to trucks and was working loading food, and I was third in the family. When I grew up they put me in the dormitory. My father and mother they didn't have much.

They had no homes, they lived in a wind break. The dorm had a home and school, government school and dancing. They were Catholic used to live there, you know?

When my father stopped working he started stealing sheep. When the police got him they chained him up, chained his ankles. It was very sad to see him walking around like that. He had to walk like that from Halls Creek to Wyndham.

In the school when I was older, I used to play with Melda and Gracie. Those nuns taught us everything. We used to work very hard doing the washing. Sometimes we used to run out of water. We'd go to the well and none would come up. We'd all cry for water. That's why we moved to New Balgo. It's called Wirrimanu.

When we all settled down in New Balgo there was too much grog in Papunya and so they moved them to Balgo in 1974. Too much grog and too much fighting so they moved them. Well when they got there they discovered that they were all family. And they were so happy to see each other – they'd come from north, east, south and west to be in Balgo, see? And they all were related! Hugging them, crying; they'd been playing together in the desert when they were little kids.

In 1982 they moved back to Kiwirrkurra. The government asked them if they wanted to move back and they did. They moved back to their sacred place, to look after their country. And my mother moved back to Kiwirrkurra – they were so happy to go back. That's why we go up and down, you know, to visit. Because we're all scattered around. It's good – they're home. Palya.

My father was a young man living in Gordon Downs (Ringer Soak) when kartiya came in the truck to take them to school in Alice Springs. He jumped off the truck in the Tanami desert. His family found him. He later told me he wished he had stayed on the truck and went to school, because he could of learned to drive a truck. He told me, 'I shouldn't have run away, but I thought they were gonna kill me'.

Elizabeth Noonie Nangala Lulu

Hi, my name is Elizabeth Noonie Nangala Lulu. I was born at Billiluna Station. My mum she would go to work every day for the white stockmen, washing clothes and keeping the station area neat and tidy. She was single mother living with mother and father. Then one day old man (Eddie Calyen) was a truck driver bringing in loading for the station. He fell in love with my mother (Veronica Lulu), then they were moving around Billiluna, took us from station to station looking for work. We came back to Billiluna, lived there for a while. Then we had to move to Balgo. Our parents had to take us for school at Balgo Mission. We the Walmajarri mob was living at the corner of bottom camp with our families. Then two old men, my grandfather Tiger and Lucky, were telling story about their country (Lake Gregory) Mulan. They would talk to their sons, Rex Johns, Don Pelican, Ronnie Ronalds, telling them about this Walmajarri Country, Lake Gregory, Mulan, then they went talking to the father Ray Hevern, then they went to Canberra Parliament House to get their country back, then we Walmajarri mob moved here to our country with our Walmajarri old people in Mulan and Billiluna. Now we are happy living in our land. I grew up at the dormitory at Balgo because my family were here at Mulan. Me and my sister Karen, we were going to school at Balgo, come every Fridays for weekends spend time with families. I was always camping with my grandmother and grandfather, then my grandmother was telling story about her country Wangkatjunka land Walkali. Then I was asking her, so you came from other country, from Wangkatjunka Country, because I didn't know she was from Walkali Broome College (Nulungu). Then I started asking my grandfather where they met, where they were living before they met. They met at Lake Stretch (Nyarna). Anyways, my grandmother was a kind and helpful woman, looked after grandfather very much because my grandfather was a blind man. He was a strong culture man, always talking about his dreaming story about his country. That why my home is Paruku, Lake Gregory, Mulan. I found my Desert Dreaming of Walmajarri and Wangkajunka, great-grandfather from Kurrnyiji and Jaru. Then when I finish my school I started helping my mother painting about country and getting stories from all of my grandfather and grandfather's brother's stories and grandmother's stories and how they would move around this country gathering bush tucker, visiting families. Now my family are still here at Mulan and my grandfather family are at Billiluna, Halls Creek, Ringer Soak, Fitzroy Crossing. My grandmother from Christmas Creek. My family are mixed with family from Broome, Derby from my husband Fernandez family, Marshall and more. My life here in the desert is a good happy life. Sometimes sadness come into my life, but I don't like being sad, I like to enjoy life with happiness, sharing stories with my family and friends. I like going out bush trip, camping with my family or friends. My children are four sons, two daughters, seven grandchildren. I love them all with all my heart. No matter where they are I still remind them where their Dreaming history comes from, great-grandfather and great-grandmothers from the Desert Dreaming history. My children are connected with Sea Dreaming from their father family from Broome and Derby.

EL: Spray, with water, and squirt them through the window.

KM: Just like the dogs.

EL: Go, Wirra, go home. You've got school tomorrow. Next day they didn't turn up for school! And we would know that they'd been both— .

KM: It's generational, isn't it? Chasing the boys.

EL: I had this set of fun time. I moved to Perth and made more boyfriends. They were kartiya boys. And my hormones started to change and I said, 'No, I got to find the right man'.

KM: How did you find your right man?

EL: I was in Perth and I was walking there, making fun with my other friends and plus my friends from same college from Broome, they were there, from Derby, Bidyadanga, Broome, and I came back and find him here in Mulan.

KM: You grew up together, did you?
EL: Yeah. It was like a set-up date. It wasn't my choice, you know.

KM: Who set you up?

EL: They said, 'They'll match, let's set them up'. They came and asked me and I was listening to ABBA music that I was listening to.

KM: 'Fernando'?

EL: 'Tin Shed'. You know that house where Rebecca is? Well next door is tin shed. That was my grandmother's tin shed house and the next one was Bessie's and I was in there listening to music, and they came up and slung rock. It was late. Not really late. And they asked me, 'So-and-so want to see you', and I said, 'What? No!' I was really scared and they forced me there. They really wanted me to go. So I said, 'All right'. I didn't want to hurt their feelings.

KM: And the rest is history! Did you see him around? Did you think, 'Oh he's good looking'?

EL: Yeah, I used see him. I used to stand in that house with the binoculars spying where he is. I found these binoculars and I thought, 'Hey! What is this doing here? I'll use them, spy on where he is'. In the single quarters. You know where the new building is? The new house that was built? Just behind Jamie's house, yeah, there used to be single quarters there. And I was spying on a man.

Veronica Lulu

My name is Veronica Lulu. I will talk about the desert life, how I grew up in the desert with my family, how my mother and father used to live. My family is spread out. I was born on the lake place called Gun-gun-ga near Lake Stretch. I was born there. I was born first of July in 1952. And I was staying in Lake Stretch, there was bit more people came in from the desert, from everywhere, big girls and a little baby there. And after when people move out to other communities – Balgo, Sturt Creek, Fitzroy – I went up to Wangkajungka and Fitzroy. All my people from the desert from Walkali, from Wangkajungka they went up to stay somewhere to work. And after that we shift to Billiluna because we had no food there and not good water at Lake Stretch. So we went to Billiluna. Those days, was called Yarri. We went there. And still lot of peoples was there and I was a kid there, in Billiluna, my people used to work there. Old people come to there from the desert. And some cousins went away to other communities. Some families went away to Lake Gregory, Balgo, Fitzroy, Sturt Creek, Gordon Downs, Hall's Creek; some went to Kununurra. All went away.

And some still were there: my mother and father was still there, my brother and sister was there, because there's a good life for us to live and knowledge. That's how we learn through our country, to keep it strong, and our language and culture, and we pass it on to young people. Yeah. My mother and father took me to Fitzroy, and I came back to Hall's Creek, but mostly I stayed in my country, Billiluna, and we had rough time with manager, and we went to Balgo, to other families. We stayed there in Balgo for couple of years and then my brothers and old people was talking about this lake, this desert lake, Lake Gregory. Government gave us back.

That's how we got this desert lake and Mulan, our community and how we run it. That's how we keep our young people knowledge and to learn more about it, to our desert, to go hunting. Food, bush tucker, some water, rockhole: how our old people used to live. And we passed this on to young people, how to live in their land. My home, my town. I go to other communities but I still come back to desert. Even my kids, they all here; they go and come back to desert. Good life, desert. Not the town or city. All here, they come back. And desert is a good life for young people to learn their knowledge and everything. And we do a painting. Yeah, bush tucker, bush medicine, knowledge, stories, hunting, language, and how to hunt and find food.

Like the early days our ancestors used to do, we still do this looking after country forever. This is our home for us: desert. Touch me, my spirit in desert, make me strong, make me well. When I go town, no good. I lose it. Knowledge and strength and power. Desert brings it back, gives me strength and power to live, and learn my young people.

My bush name is Kanpirr. That's a bush medicine.

That's how I learn my young people. My grandchildren, my

great-grandchildren, my daughters and sons, niece and nephew, I learn them; I taught them.

Well I got too much grandchildren, too much, from my sons and daughters.

But great-grandchildren, I got thirteen.

I'm sixty-three now. And I'm still working for my country.

And I'm happy here, in the desert in Lake Gregory. But I travel. I been to Singapore, Samoa, Perth, Canberra, Middle East, Rome, Jerusalem. Meeting lot of people, different people from different countries. Yeah, I took my story, even to Alice Springs, I went, painting, telling people about my country, where I come from. But I still come back to my country, that's my spirit, that's my people. And I feel happy when I do painting. I can't go without painting for my country. Painting make me, give me strength and power. For my old people, how they used to live. Our old people used to walk and sleep and live on the land and hunt. For this lake, my father's country.

Even I do the same for my mother country, you know? But when I go to my mother country, first time, I cry. Long way. South of Balgo. South of Yagga-yagga. When I seen it I think of my children and grandchildren. It was special, my mother and grandfather and grandmother country.

I told KL and Noonie, 'That's your grandmother country'.

People go together. They move around, go camp from camp. Mothers, fathers, they were here. My father, he was here. My father was this country. We cry.

My mother found my father. He couldn't see her because he was blind.

She passed away in '68. He passed away '97.

Karen Lulu

Our dormitory. Swimming at Balgo. Swimming from Monday to Friday, Friday go back to Mulan. When we go back, the old people take us out, hunting for bush tucker, but not with vehicle, but walking the way we used to go. Round that way, walking, with a little billycan. Go looking round everywhere for bush tomato, from Parnkupirti but other side. Looking around. Sometimes the old people take us for bush potato. They used to take us on weekends. On Sunday after church, we go back on the vehicle that was available to Balgo for school. From there, I went to school in Balgo then to Nulungu College, in Broome.

We all went to Broome. Robin, Rhonda, Rebecca Johns, Phillipa. Some come from Balgo and Billiluna, we all meet family, come together in Broome. It was good schooling there, but some girls were getting cheeky to us: 'You can't sit there, that's our bus'.

They were bullying and teasing Sometimes we run away from school, because too much bullying. We run away to the town, but we go back, and go working, like workforce. Clean the school area, like gardening and raking. A punishment. Not to do that again.

We went camping out to Willagee Gorge, near Fitzroy. We got there, and the girls were a bit cheeky too. We had a little meeting, what to do. Some of the girls said that when the sun goes down we go to Fitzroy, walking. So, when the sun went down we start walking to Fitzroy. Philippa Guguman said, 'I've got a father there, we could stay for the night there'.

We all went there together. We walked when the sun going down. Maybe six or seven o'clock. Walking in the dark to Fitzroy.

From there, we got up early in the morning ready to go, get a lift to Hall's Creek. We got up and walked to the bridge. We went there and we stayed under the bridge area. But we had no water. We stayed quite a while and one girl said, 'No, I need to go have shower'.

'OK, we can go back.'

So we went back and we asked this other girl from Christmas Creek, 'Did you see the bus?'

'Yeah, I seen that bus; it gone back to Broome', she told us.

We went back to town and we seen this bus coming, it hadn't gone to Broome. It was still looking around.

The woman bus driver told uncle, 'Those young girls, they run away'. We was walking past a supermarket, walked past there, and we seen this big bus coming. And they all scared, all the girls, they all scared of it. But the woman put the brake down and got off, 'Come here, all you girls! Naughty girls for running away'.

So we got on the bus and went back to Broome. The next day they gave us workforce for running away.

Then our grandmother passed away. So the families told us, those ones that are in Broome, they need to come back. All the kids. Rebecca, Jeffery, Francis—

They need to come back for their grandmother.

And we told the school, 'We're going. We're going back to Mulan'. Those other mob cry, 'I want to go too!' We told the people in charge, the ones looking after us, we told them, 'They're family too. They have to come'. So we all went.

I've got two girls, I've got six grandkids.

I would like my grandkids to go to school and to learn more and to go to other schools so that they can learn to read and write and to earn their own money and to look after their kids. To go to other schools and to come back to Mulan to work here.

That's why I tell my grandkids, 'You need to go to school and learn'. I have two daughters and I tell them to take their kids to school when they're young. Little kids learn more. They like to go to school.

I want my grandkids to learn to read and write, to learn white society. Both ways.

I didn't go to more school. I stayed back home, you know. I'm sorry about that.

They had adult education in school, long time ago. But it stopped. No more teachers teaching older people.

Evelyn Clancy and Kim Mahood

EC: I'm Evelyn Clancy. My mother is from Ngalia tribe. All the way, travelling. Young girl. Right after Mangkayi. My big sister there.

KM: Tell us what happened to your big sister.

EC: They kill her right there, my sister, because they was talking like that: kartiya, kartiya!

KM: So they reckon her father was a kartiya because she was too bright. Bright means light-skinned.

EC: Too bright.

KM: Do you think he was a kartiya or she was just bright colour?

EC: Bright. Bright colour. He not my father.

KM: So he was light-skinned as well. She was light-skinned and they reckoned kartiya father. Ah, so when she was big one they—

EC: Choked her. My father was working. Cutting timber for yards at Kururrungku.

KM: On the river. And that's your Dreaming isn't it? Water Snake.

EC: Water Snake. Growing up. My aunt even take me, no?

KM: Father's sister. So what happened to your mother?

EC: She leave. After that she pass away.

Father found another woman now. Took her to Sturt Creek.
But he was staying there, in Jalyuwarn.
My aunty would tell me 'bout donkey. Donkey been buck me and my mother.
We been fall off. Get up and laugh.
Right up to Carranya.
We stopped long time.

River there – old people is staying there. Aunties, uncles. Families, you know? We grew up all there. Swimming there at Carranya.
Flick, flick – a little fly. Night-time.

KM: What is it? A glow worm? A firefly?

EC: Yeah. Good feed.

KM: You ate fireflies?

EC: No. The tree where they stop got little fruit, *kirnti*, like a plum, like a conkerberry.

Hunting all day. Old people they spear kangaroo. Take him back to camp. Then go for dingo. The whole day catching dingos. Kill them. Cook them.

KM: So you had cooked dingo?

EC: Not dingo, not really dingo, what do they call them?

KM: Camp dog.

EC: Camp dog, no, not dingo…fox…when they told me, I vomited.

KM: You vomited? When you heard that it was fox? Even though it tasted alright?

EC: Tasted right, like pussycat.

KM: So this is all along the river? Sturt Creek.

EC: Riverside…that's where we grow up. Emu egg, mussel, witchetty grub…and parrot.

KM: You ate parrot? What sort of parrot?

EC: Cocky, kiling-kiling.

KM: Galah. So how did you eat them? Did you cook them in coals?

EC: Yeah.

Then from there my husband come up...

I ran away. Up and run away from there.

KM: *Where did you run?*

EC: Right up to rubbish tip, come back again night time.

My aunty walking, my mother climb up on saddle, and me in front.

Strong one, my aunty, strong one. Asleep and rocking away. Rock me to sleep.

Working in the garden and the laundry at Sturt Creek, washing and ironing.

I went to Billiluna with my husband. I been findem Megan first, then Leonard, last one Leanne. Leanne been born on the doctor plane. Yep...three kids now.

Went to Balgo and come back again. From there we come here to Mulan and we stay here long time now. For good now.

That's all? No more stories about me.

KM: *What about that time you showed me at Billiluna pool where there was a big fight?*

EC: Oh yeah, long time. From Balgo come big fight there. I was running round, got a boomerang.

KM: *So what was the fight about?*

EC: I don't know. Some girl maybe.

KM: Somebody told me that might have been about you that fight?

EC: No, no, no, long time. Even different language fighting there.

From here, from Warmun, from Sturt Creek, all them fighting, people wanna rob the wives, and from that they fight.

Stealing wives.

Leonard Boxer

Born in Wyndham. My name is Leonard Boxer. And I went to Sturt Creek when I was eleven, twelve. Then I went to Hooker Creek. From Hooker Creek I went back to Sturt Creek. Sturt Creek to Halls Creek. Halls Creek back to Ringers Soak. Back to Sturt Creek. Went back to Halls Creek. Went back to Billiluna. From Billiluna went to Balgo. From Balgo went back to Billiluna, and from Billiluna went back to Mulan. And stay in Mulan for long time.

Went to school in Halls Creek.
Somewhere, somewhere for four or five years, somewhere…

I just grow up there, grow up there. Sometime we were running away from teacher in Sturt Creek.

Getting all the gum in the tree. Yeah.

I was running back to the yards. Branding. I was gunna be a young stockman.

Yeah. I was young feller running away from house in Sturt Creek. Went to the yard, get one bridle, one horse, get Biscuit. Get a chair to get on the horse.

Yeah. Walked him to the yard, stayed on the horse. And that horse, its name is Biscuit.

Yeah cause I was running away from this school. Running away from this yard.

Bang, straight to bush.

Well in the bush you can see everything. You got a lot of bush food and there's freedom out there.

I went to Balgo, yeah. I was schooling there.

Ahh, different, well, like, another world out there you know? Yeah. Another big world you know.

When I was growing up, when I start living older life. A lot of different language. Yeah.

My first language is Jaru. Then I was talking Walmajarri. Little bit Ngalia.

Cause I can't quite get that language correct. But most us speak little bit Warlpiri when all the family come in.

I can still speak them language. And good English too.

Sometimes when I go out there, sometime I cry.

Because I grew up there, Sturt Creek. When I went past, to Ringers Soak, passing through suddenly I would cry, cry all the time.

Just go back there, maybe go for kangaroo or hunting.

Sometime I wouldn't go to town, too much party. I'm not alcoholic.

My grandfather used to chop all the trees and work in the yard. My grandfather, they call him Mutaka (Motorcar).

He was bush mechanic. My grandfather, Motorcar Man.

Same as my other brother who passed away.

We should get the boys together in Mulan, to run the station properly. I wanna see this thing happen. One more time you know. I wanna see all the cattle in the yard there. And all the horse.

Yeah. Well when we got manager here, Geoffrey, I don't know when he gonna start. That's why I'm waiting for Geoffrey. Yeah.

I don't know what I'm going to do now. I'm go and work in the cemetery, or work in the garden.

I wanna see everything here. Like, I wanna do this oval, put all them lights, and that band area, go and chuck all them sand in there, for the dancing ground.

Yeah. I wanna see that happen.

Yeah I'll go and see Hanson and they boys, go and see them, and help with them.

Well they need to listen properly in the school. Listen to kids, listen to teacher, and listen to the old people...Yeah.

From Sturt Creek I went to Mongrel Downs. I was working there. Then, with Malley Brown in Homestead.

A lot of bush woman in there, back in Ngulupi and Mongrel Downs.

My uncle always chuck me on the horse all the time. In Mongrel Downs, Sturt Creek. Yeah.

My other uncle he was working there in Mongrel Downs too.

Yeah I was working with Mally Brown there in Homestead,

then I went to Mongrel Downs, Patrick was there too. Patrick Kopp he was working in Mongrel Downs.

Yeah, I was working with Patrick Kopp. He was the head stockman.

Patrick was talking, 'You know how to ride a horse?' I told Patrick nah, you gotta learn me, but I didn't tell him I got my own yard, in here, got my own school.

Yeah, my brother passed away. He was another rider again, we used to come out riding in saddle bronc in Homestead rodeo, but he was killing all the horse.

Yeah…a lot of blood, from the spurs. Yeah, a lot of blood. Very bad, straight in the yard. Kill one horse, kill another one. Straight through.

Rodeo. Yeah, in Homestead.

Whitefella put us from Sturt Creek. We decided to go. Go all away. Moved from Sturt Creek to Maddox. It's got a lake in there too. From Maddox, went to Red Rock. All around that area. Yeah. No toilet. Nothing.

Living off the land. You know the land.

From Red Rock, went to Karranya.

Have to go Palm Springs one day, paradise. Looking from right on the top there. Paradise.

Up the top, big swim pool there for the Aboriginal kids. And another one there with Rainbow Snake. We don't swim in that other one, we swim in the top one.

Yeah. Take you there one day.

Mununga.

They will find you first.
They were all coming closer.

Ask who this? Who that white, white woman in there. They are mununga. We call mununga. Long hair, right down to ground. And they use their own hair to cover themselves.

All the boys, all the men, if they stick together, they grab bush woman. And they put it in the smoke.
All their hair fall off.
And they turn into white woman. Right, so they stop being bush woman and they become good wife or something.
Yeah their hair all fall out.

They after man. They chasing man, yes.
If man run into the bush, you can see bush banana rolling. Behind you. Behind the horse. You'll see another bush tucker. Behind you. Chasing you, ah.

You can gallop faster, yeah, if you want. Well, you can get off and decide.
You can't out-run them.

Yeah, blue-tongue. Kill the blue-tongue and cook it up and eat it up. I'll be a boyfriend to the girl if I cook it up.

Dugar had one bush woman.
Remember Dugar? He was working here.

The bush woman there, she say, 'I want me and you to go together'.

In homestead, baby cry, the baby cry, and the men start listening, oh they coming now for men, they turned the power off, in homestead and Mongrel Downs.

One little baby. Don't cry because bush woman here. Right in front of us.

They come for men. Hair is red. Red ochre.
   Yeah.

[*Evelyn Clancy joins the discussion*]

EC: They make noise like that. Julyu-julyu, julyu-julyu.

KM: What makes noise? The girl? Make it again; make that sound.

EC: Julyu-julyu, julyu-julyu. Little girl spirits.

KM: You can hear them out in the bush doing that?

EC: You can hear them coming closer and closer.

KM: That sounds like birds.

EC: Like when baby cry. They put the julyu-julyu in the handbag, to make it quiet.

EC: My father Clancy killing bush man now. Run from some-where, from Red Rock. They would kill him. Right up to Weedy Lake. From Weedy Lake came back for same man.

Walking in circles. Keep coming back to the body.

KM: So who's been killed?

EC: Bushman. Right round right round and my father come back again...biting him there, you know.

KM: So who bit him?

EC: My father.

KM: I know where you're telling me he bit him. But, was it your father got bitten?

EC: No. That dead man. My father bite his balls off. Spit it out. So he can, go, go back to his home.

KM: That's how he had to get away from that dead Featherfoot.

EC: Yeah he was walking in circles.

KM: Ah, so he was trapped walking in circles? Because of Featherfoot? So even dead Featherfoot could make him walk around in circles? That's a pretty bad thing you've gotta do to get free.

LB: Walking in circles.

I gotta get out of this circle!

How I get from here?

He thought he might kill him.

Because he might come for him again. So he thinks, 'Oh yeah, I forgot'.

Went back there, bite his balls off and turn around and walk away....

The old people remember stories; make them kids sleep.

KM: Yeah. Make the kids sleep. I reckon it will wake them up. Keep them awake! Bad dreams.

LB: Kids today want story.

KM: So do you still tell kids stories like that?

LB: No I didn't. Other stories.

KM: So what sort of stories would you tell kids today?

LB: Fishing…picnic…Across the water and back.

Bessie Doonday

(This is an edited excerpt from *The Children of Tiger Wirirr*,
published by the Kimberley Language Resource Centre.)

We were all living in Balgo when we started talking for this
country. My brother Rex asked the old men, Tiger and Lucky,
'Where can we find a place for ourselves to live? We are all here
at Balgo and we've got nowhere to go. We've been wandering
around everywhere looking for a place to live, in our country'.

'Ah', Tiger and Lucky said, 'Your place is down there,
it's Lake Gregory. Mulan is your country, that's the country
belonging to you. And Kururrungku (Billiluna), too, belongs to
you. That's the place you can speak up for. That's the country
belonging to you lot'.

So we stayed at Balgo a little while longer. Then one day
John Eadie told my brother and the others the good news that
these two stations, Billiluna and Lake Gregory, were for sale.
Later on the stations were bought for our mob and we all came
here to Mulan to live. We were living there with no houses,
only a garage, a big house, a storeroom, a singles house and a
little bit of a toilet. We used to sleep outside. Only the manager
used to sleep in the house – my brother Rex and his wife, Anna,

and their family. They used to say to us, 'You can come and join us'. When we first came we had nothing. We only had four little tents and some houses made out of corrugated iron.

Old man Lucky passed away at Balgo before we moved to Mulan. So other old men brought us to this country, these three, my father Tiger, Dinny Brown and Boxer Billiluna (Jalaku). Those three brothers. Kilampi Pye is another brother, but he came later. That's the end of the story that I've been telling about the old men and us finding our country.

People came from everywhere, from Ringers Soak, some of them from Balgo and Kururrungku, Halls Creek, Yagga Yagga and some of them from here for the 'hand-over' meeting. And old Sandy Cox's mob came from the Fitzroy area. And from Derby too they came. We are the traditional owners. We talked about it and the kartiya put sand in our hands and all that kind of thing. We sang a corroborree for them. They all clapped for us. We had got the land back, no? And we are living on this country today. They gave us our country, Native Title. They gave us back this country.

Shirley Yoomarie

I used to live around Sturt Creek. Little one. This priest came
and took us now to the mission. Now we went to Billiluna
first. Went to Billiluna first with my family, stopped there in
the blue house. But I was always with Shirley Brown, hanging
around, playing at her grandfather's house. And then, they was
letting me to sleep there, because they had all the toys and
everything.

Yes, with her grandparents. Always playing around. Get all
the hay in the chook yards. We used to go over there in the
morning, we used to throw the eggs, steal the eggs. And the
grandparents, they were waiting, wanting their breakfast – you
know, eggs?

Me and Shirley, we used to go and steal the eggs all the
time. So I'd go and run. Yeah, all the eggs gone! All the young
people were there: May, Noonie, Bessie mob. When they had
cattle, and nanny goat, horses and chook yard. We had all those
around there.

McGuire, Father McGuire, you know? 'Kids going to go to
school now.'

We used to get on the truck and cry all the way to Balgo.

They take me, little one, five years old.

I never used to see my parents – I used to come to holiday, that's all. When I finished, when I was finishing school, I was still hanging around because I got used to that dormitory. I used to hang around there, when I had my first child, Anne-Marie.

When I was young, about seventeen, I had first child. Seventeen, yeah. I didn't have anywhere, hospital or anywhere. It was in the dormitory.

The nuns sent me up to Wyndham now. I came back and I went to Billiluna. Then back to Balgo. We was in Balgo now, staying there for good. My sister was just married. Gracie Mosquito – full sister, from one mother but different father. She got married. The nuns promised me, 'You two can stay because you got little girl'. So we both stayed.

And I find my husband now. We both stayed and I had another girl, another boy. We went back to Billiluna now.

When I was little bit big my family used to take us to Ruby Plains. My mother used to take us to Ruby Plains and work there. Me and Steven was there – me, Steven, Launa and Peter, that's all. And a kartiya was giving out, every morning, breakfast. Just to go and get all the sheeps and bring them back. We used to round them up. 'Go get those sheeps and you can have breakfast in the morning.'

I was all the time with family, following the family all around. We was staying in Balgo and we moved through Ngulupi Homestead with our families. With Ronnie and Nora and all that family.

All the wives was there, all the Darkies (their surname) was there. They was all there living in the house. We moved away from the homestead back to Balgo. And that old Rex was asking the Father for us to go back to our country. And they gave a little paper, permission. Country there, you know? You better go back.

My grandfather Lucky told Tiger Wirirr, 'Take all them kids to the Walmajarri country. Go back.'

He passed away in Balgo. Lucky, he passed away in Balgo, he know that his country was here. And we all went and followed old man Tiger to this place. They had a little tin house – little kartiya house, fridge outside, little freezer and little stock thing, saddle, you know?

We came here. Paper, white like this, signed, all the old people: signing, signing, signing, all the old people, to get this place back.

All my old people gone now, and I'm still here.

Looking after my grandchildren now, today. Two here and another four over there, somewhere. Another five over there in Balgo.

My father is Walmajarri and my mother is Ngalia and my grandmother is a Ngalia and my grandfather is Walmajarri.

I should talk Walmajarri, really.

My mother from Jaru and Ngalia.

I'm from three different tribes. Married for thirty years with my husband. When he passed away, last one. I'm still here with my grandchildren.

No more husbands. No more.

From daughters, son, I got maybe nine grandchildren.

I need to lock my son away. Go away, no more kids!

Wendy Chungulla

This here is our grandfather country (Kimiti Wallaby), is called Paruku, and this is Walmatjarri country and he is Walmatjarri man.

Long time ago he lived on the lake where he stayed with his wife, kids and sisters and brother and all his other families. They used to walk around the lake looking and hunting for food. Kimiti had five wives. First one was Jajudd; he had four children with her. They were Harry Chungulla, George Wallaby, Violet Campbell and Biddy Wallaby; they were the first children they had. Then later on Kimiti had his second wife; together they had Ivan Holliman and Nora Mundijerry. Later he had third wife, Tulli, then they had Mona Lightning and soon later on he had married a woman from Derby side, then they had Roger Burgu. Soon after Kimiti Wallaby married Daisy Yoomarie. They had Jimmy Smith and Gracie Mosquito then they were all living at Lake Stretch that used to be called Bililuna Station, Old Bililuna Station. And the first Harry Chungulla was born at Lake Stretch and the rest of Kimiti children, they all born around Lake Gregory and Lake Stretch area. That's why we all care about Bililuna and Mulan Lake. Harry's children was born somewhere else but they still lived on Bililuna where Kimiti Wallaby and Jajudd is buried now also along with our other grandfather Boxepiggy piggy and Jaja Poyul. We don't know where our own Jaja Gnarmpan is buried, maybe in Balgo.

Gladys was born on 1 July 1901 at Ghardadubiddi between Lake Gregory and Bililuna Station. She was the only child of Boxer and Gnarmparn. Gladys grew up around Bililuna area. She used to walk around the countryside like Sturt Creek, Bililuna, Ruby Plains. At that time there wasn't any vehicle to take them around to place. When she was ten years old she used to live at Palm Springs with her grandparents. Her father used to let her stay with them. Later on she moved on to Lake Stretch. That's where she found her husband, Harry Chungulla. They got married at an early age. Form there they moved to Ruby Plains, then to Lamboo Station. That's when they had they first son Raymond, was born at Lamboo Station. Then they moved to Bow River Station. Later they had their second son, Tony, there. On they moved to Argyle Down Station, they had John, then Reggie and Wendy and Susan.

Cathy Lee

In the early days I was taken away from my parents, staying with other girls. Then other girls came from Sturt Creek Station and Gordon Downs Station who came with Father Hevern. He put the station girls in the dormitory. Sister Philomena asked the Balgo girls to look after them, but when the station girls told Sister Philomena that they had their own language, Jaru, Sister Philomena said: 'Don't use languages in the dormitory. You speak English only'.

The sisters used to teach us after school to say our Hail Mary and rosary before going to church. On Sundays we walked in a line to church. Every Sunday wearing a white dress, they'd say to us: 'You have to scrub with soap and use scrubbing brush'.

We had to wash our own dress and we weren't allowed to go in public with the other girls and boys – we had to stay at the dormitory.

Every afternoon Sister Philomena used to take us out to Jesus' Cave at the lookout to say a quiet prayer or rosary with the other girls.

Imelda Gugaman

In Martu my families came all the way from desert. I was child, my father carry me on his back and my mother was pregnant. We walking at night, we stay, have a rest and have sleep. In the morning we start walk again, but the people found lots of bush tomatoes. Then we came to Mulan. We stay for a night and mother gave birth. Aunty told, 'You have brother Richard, he was born in Mulan'. My baby brother was crying, crying my mother was, but sick, she left my little brother to die, so Josephine ran back, got the baby. My father said to her look after the baby. In the morning Maggie's father, Anne's father, Raymond's father spear one bullock, they cut bullock with the stone so they all cook the meat, we all had good feast. After we had lunch we went to Balgo. The nun talked to the dormitory sister, she put cloth and ribbon on my hair. My little brother was in the clinic, nuns were looking after my little brother.

My mother she was young when she came to Balgo with my father. My father was married with Lucy and Lumpiya. In '60 my father died, she was a single. She used to look after me and Richard. In '68 she was married to Joey Chungari so the first child born was Joseph, then Kathy, Raymond, Carmel, Christine. And Daniel. In '64 we were at the dormitory. We did not have much food. At night we go stealing at night. But anyhow, we had good time going out for picnic.

My mother was telling me a story. When I was a little baby, about twelve months old, they used to dig a hole in the sand and cover me up to keep me cool. Me and Jossie in old man's country Jupiter. Well, when I was five or six years old Josephine was our babysitter when my parents were going hunting. Grandparents were with us too.

One day a pilot came along in a helicopter and left a container with oil and Dad and uncles were painting us with oil, all black. Jossie and me all sitting in the shade waiting for that pilot to come back. Some was still left in the drum. He came back and calling out and we stood up all covered in black oil. He got a shock. I think he got a fright. Yuwayi.

When they first saw that helicopter they were throwing spears. When they was going droving with camel and they were running fast to hide from those kartiyas. Hide underneath those bushes and she tell us not to make a noise. I was about five or six or seven years old, scared. They might have shot us. Some sad stories. When my mother first saw the white people with the rifle and saw them shooting and killing them, you know. That was very sad. That was my family. Some were young ones and some were pregnant. This is what my mother told me. Her mother used to tell her, 'When you see them you hide from them'.

So the pilot was the first good one. He used to bring flour and meat for them. Yuwayi.

They called my father 'government'. Why people calling him that? Because his skin was fair colour. That's where they get that from. Yuwayi.

On Saturdays, you know Saturday morning used to go to dining room, wash the table in the morning when it's finished. Instead of mopping the floor we'd kneel down and scrub the floor. In those days – no mops. Polish the floor. Wash pots and pans and dishes and knives and forks. Hard job.

We were stealing apricots and pears. Eating quickly if a sister comes along. Those days were really hard for us. Scrubbing, washing, putting wood in the stove for fire. It was chopped already. We had to get the fire ready.

When sister comes she start making supper and we put plates on the table ready. Yuwayi.

Some of us were eating apricots, but Nita she had the tin and she opened it and her hand got stuck in the tin and we hear the sister coming and I said, 'Quick, the sister is coming', but her fingers were stuck and she was hiding her hand down like this. The sister says, 'What is this with your hand? Oh I've caught you red-handed'. And we were in the toilet laughing. She didn't get any supper. Yowie.

Some of the ladies were hiding bread underneath their pants. We didn't get much food. We were starving.

Lizzie and her future husband were kissing in the window dormitory. He came in through the window. And the sister was coming. He tried to get out but he got stuck in the window. His legs got stuck in the bar. Yowie.

That special night we had crackers and Gracie and me and Eva were walking. Rooster was chasing Eva from stealing her eggs. And we were all saying, 'Hurry up, hurry up, where's those eggs?'

Helicopter had a mirror to shine and signal to Lucy in the dormitory. She was young, in her thirties. He was a cheeky one.

Susan Chungulla

Born on Argyle Station in 1963, and left Argyle, left my mother and family in 1969. I moved to Queensland, living on outback cattle stations with my adopted family. My adopted mother and father have since passed on now.

My mother, Gladys Chungulla, and my brother and sisters met me and my first-born children, Philip and Andrew, in Kurrungku 1988 for the first time.

Coming back home was incredibly emotional experience, sad and happy and very overwhelming.

Through the coming years, I gradually started learning and reconnecting with all my families in the Kimberleys, my grandfather Kimiti Wallaby and grandmother Gnarmpan.

Along the way I have learnt a lot about the bush medicines, bush tuckers and stories carried by my grandparents to me and my family. It is a very free, happy life living and travelling around in the desert. The lakes and sandy hills and grassy spinifex country has so much to offer me, spiritually and physically. 'Being on country' gives me a lot of pride and strength.

Tiffany

Hi, I'm Tiffany, I grew up in Mulan since I was a baby. I will never forget this beautiful community. It has always been my home; this is where I feel comfortable with everyone I know. We who live in Mulan were all a big happy family. It doesn't really matter when people fight sometimes, but we always forgive one another. But we must try and help others to start working again, helping kids to go to school every day so they can take over our places and make us proud!

Mulan has a big lake sometimes. When it's a hot summer day we always go out enjoy the outback, but what I want is to have a better future for new generation.

Moses Obah

My father Philip Obah was born on Palm Island to Wilfred Obah and Rachel May Sullivan. My father's maternal grandfather is a Madja man from Forrest Hill near Woorbinda on the Blackdown Tablelands.

My father's paternal grandfather was born on Obah Island – Vanuatu – in the South Sea Islands and was sent to Palm Island after cane cutting in North Queensland.

My mother's family and grandfather (Kimiti Wallaby) called Paruku – this is Walmajarri country.

I have two sisters, Daisy and Myra, and three brothers, Philip, Andrew and Raymond. I am the youngest of three brothers.

I am twenty-one years old and born in Townsville. I am a descendant of Wadja, Jirrabul and Mamu. Mamu is just before Cairns. I am also a descendant from Obah Island.

I have been travelling since I was young, all around the desert out here, going to different communities, and country, lakes and waterfalls.

I have been fishing and went to get fresh killer in Kurrurungku, around Lake Stretch, with my cousin brother Derek Padoon.

I enjoy driving and have driven to Mulan, Billiluna and Balgo. We have travelled to Two Tree – Giji. My mum Bessie Doonday took me down to the water and washed my arms, legs and head to welcome me back to country.

I felt happy and made my spirit strong and happy. I didn't know properly this great grandfather's country, Kimiti Wallaby.

I caught fish straight away as I threw my line out, and cooked and ate the fish on the fire.

Littlies at Mulan School 2013

Talia

I look horse and camel on the road heading for lake.
  We look another horse when we go river.

Sebanna

I go to Broome. I get a lolly. I jump on the mail plane to go
Broome.
  We been go to second hand and get thongs and clothes.

Tamati

I go to the part of the lake and saw how big it used to be and
saw clam shells. We drove down it in the truck. My dad broke
the tree over with a chainsaw.

Dakota

We was going to the lake. Me and mum and dad were going
fishing and my brother Desmond.

Dylan

We go to Parnkupirti for a walk with my jaja and Denisha.

Dakota

We went to Parnkupirti. We saw some leaves for food and Jessica mashed some leaves for sores.

Gracie

Hanson was telling about his painting. He was talking about the lake and he was talking about with that snake.

Tamati

We went to Parnkupirti and it was a road that went into the river and there was a big hole there and it fills up with water when it's cold. It's a big river.

Tyson

We went for a bush trip in the river. We see some rocks. Hanson told us a story. The water goes to the lake.

Matthius

The lake with no water. The snake was gone with no water.

The mum look at the lake, there was no water and they went to Parnkupirti.

Diona

We went to old mission and we saw old kitchen roof and door. Kupuyu (great grandmother) was small there. We looked at old mission school. We saw a tank with no water.

Grace

Me and Dakota was going to swimming. We do biggest power in the lake.

Me and Dakota was in the boat and we was going back to home. We go into the boat and we saw one snake in the river. A little one black snake was swimming. He trying to bite a boat. The snake move the boat. We was grabbing at meat.

Middle School children at Mulan School 2013

Mulan is a community in West Australia. We live in a hot land. There is a place in the creek name Parnkupirti and it is a sacred place, the past is. Hanson his people came from the creek, they catch fish with spear, and they hunt for goanna and he told us about Walmajarri. Hanson told us to get leaves and camping out with my family out to the lake and in there we hunt for goanna and swan eggs and even go swimming and my big brother swim across the lake and he saw a big goanna, but the goanna was first.

John-John

We went to the creek. We cross over the creek. We let a Nissan in the dry mud. We was walking to the sandhill. We got a shovels and we dig it all the way. It fell down when we dig it. We dig a big hole and we got a frog put in a box. We made a fire. We burn. We cooked them in Mulan. And we cook it. We ate it and we were talking story. You know that house. Next to Mark's House. Dermott's House. We eating some frogs. Finished.

Theo Fernandez

On my holidays in Mulan I like to go shooting out with my friends. We went to Parnkupirti to listen to Hanson what this land really means. He was teaching us about Walmajarri and different names for the plants. He tell us the story of the old people. When I grow up I want to be a inventor. I forgot what I wanted to invent but I'll remember it soon. I like to invent a go-cart with big engines and a steering wheel and roll bars with controls. And glasses so you can see inside of his head when you are looking at him. And swinging ropes that can swing you like Spiderman, and it can have a spring that can jump ten metres high.

Deswan Penn

On my holiday we went to oval. We was playing footy with the man. They was playing football. Then the football was flying to me and I was running fast to the goal square. Then I kick the footy to the goal square, and we won, then we went back home and everyone was pleased. I want to play for Melbourne Demons and Swans.

Linda

On the weekend we saw some sand frogs and the mother frog died. And them little frogs were round the house. I was making a little sound and they stopped there.

Mikayley

On the weekend all the class painted the garden tank; we painted it white on every side. We are going to paint it black now.

Nathaniel

I saw a kookaburra and we hit it and we ate it. We stop and we sleep one night and we stop near the statue on the hill. We turned. We saw the bullamen. We go fishing, we go hunting, we saw the turkey, we shoot it, get a gun. That shot made my ears go deaf.

Jasmine

We went to the lake with my family, we shot a kangaroo. White-chest the dog bit the kangaroo and we took it back. We had a picnic at Kiji. Uncle Lawrence caught one fish. We ate the kangaroo and it was delicious.

Jaymin

On the weekend we played football in the soft sand. Tomorrow, the next day we catched a dingo. My dad catched it. We went back home and next day we go to swimming at Kilwa, and I swim over to the island.

The dingo came from Parnkupirti Creek where the dream-time dingoes are.

The next day me and my dad went to Kununurra for a meal and I went to my family.

Arle

On the weekend we went to Two Hill. Dad threw a big rock and we was shooting at it with small rocks. Keri, Matthius, Kelty and I had fun and then we went home.

Luke

In the weekend we went to the lake and I catched a big fish with another fishing line and I cooked it up and it was delicious, and we swim again in the water. I tell Emo to swim across the lake. We saw a duck laying some eggs and we picked up the four eggs and we swim across. We went to the bough shed. We cooked it up and put some sauce on it. It was delicious and we went back to Mulan and had some soup for dinner and we went to bed.

The End.

Kelty

On the weekend I was laughing and Kumanjayi shot the kangaroo in the leg, but it was still alive and Kumanjayi shot it in the head and it died. And we ate it in the bush and we saw a turkey and it flew away and Kumanjayi shot it and it died. We ate it later.

Dermott

One day I went to shop and I buy some drinks and bubble gum and then I went to the shop and it was close and I looked at the oval and we was playing and then we won. It was night time and we was playing at night time.

Keri

On the weekend Kelty, Arle, Matthius, Gracie and I was shooting at a ant mound. When it was my turn to shoot, I stepped right back, aimed and threw my rock at the ant mound and it broke and we went Arle's house and played on his PlayStation.

Lukie

We was playing football on the oval, all the boys, playing against each other.

Jasmine

On the weekend we went to the lake, went swimming, ate kangaroo.

Ali

Uncle Lawrence shot kangaroo, went to Kiji. The dog killed the kangaroo, the kangaroo had a joey, the dog killed joey. Ate all the kangaroo. On the way to Kiji we saw two kangaroo.

Jaymin

Dingo is living at my house in a cage. My uncle got it. Bungedi caught it there.

Keri

I saw the dingo at Ali's camp.

We made a trap for a dingo. We used half a drum for the trap, put a chain over it. We didn't put food in the drum.

Linda

We went looking for bush medicine.

John-John

On the weekend we were talking about plants. Other side of lake we saw a red car, and digged for sand frog. We caught too many.

We went to Two Hill. We were playing shoot out with the rocks. We went looking for sand frogs. Sand frog taste like chicken. Frogs were falling, falling, into a box.

Roads got muddy, could see Two Hill and lights. Got home.

Nathaniel

I like playing around, football, go swimming in the lake. Swim right across the lake to the island. We found an echidna. We saw a snake.

Mulan Senior School students at Mulan School 2013

Junior Ovi

We went from Mulan with Bush Bus to camp in Tilmouth and we camp there one night, and then we went Alice Springs on the morning. We got some McDonald's and we went to the airport and got some tickets and we flew to Melbourne. On the Sunday we went to church and then we went to see the old photos of Mulan and I was waiting because someone else was in the toilet and then I went in. When I was finished no one was there. I went to the front door but it was locked and then I went to the back door and it was open and I ran outside and a man said, 'They left on a train.' I got lost. I was running and I went round but I saw the same tree four times. Then I passed Queen Vic Market and I went to the tall tower, what's it called? The Crown Casino, and I went past and I went back to the tree and then I went to the shop; I was feeling hungry. I had $10 and I buy myself a snake lolly and I went out and saw a little church, and I went in and I prayed. After that I went back to the Queen Vic Market and I saw that park and then I was walking and I saw the train station and I went straight ahead and I saw CYC and I went in and I saw Ben and we went on the elevator and I saw Julie and Jacinta. They hugged me and then Jacinta take me back downstairs to wait for Mr Les and Miss Amy. Nigel came, he was running and he gave me a hug and he said, 'You okay?' and I said, 'Yes, I am okay'. Then the police came in and asked me about what I did, where I went and then we went to the lunchroom and we waited for lunch. After that I was full and I went back to my room and all my friends were asking me how I came back and where I went and I told them how I got lost.

The End.

Mulan Rap (group devised)

There is a place near Lake Gregory
community in Mulan and JPP
Dingo, Two Hill and Two Tree
So many things for us to see.

Turkey fly in the sky
Shoot him in the neck and then he'll die
Hunting for goanna
Cook him on the fire.

We are a tight knit community
A land of opportunity
Mulan is a place for you and me
Our people are the Walmajarri

Dingo Springs behind Two Hill
Swimming til we've had our fill
Mulan dingoes, full of mates
Training is what we do til late.

95

Emo

On my holidays in Mulan when we went to Parnkupirti and was looking for different leaves and Hanson telling story and Kim and we was getting leaves for the Walmajarri and Bessie was telling names for them. We went back to Mulan and we went to the lake and we cross over the lake and we were hunting and went back to Mulan and we go to the Two Hill and we see the lake and we go to the Dingo Springs and we went camping to Handover.

Danisha

On my holiday in Mulan community we went swimming to the lake and we went hunting and we went bush trip with Kim, and Hanson was showing the painting and he told us his story with the future and past and we got to get different plants and we got to give the plants to Bessie, and Hanson had to call the names of the plants in Walmajarri, and we had to repeat to Hanson and Jessica was grinding the bush medicine and we had to put it on our sore and we talk about our culture and opportunity. Kim had to talk about dictionary of plants and animals and check if she was right or wrong.

Terrazetta

On the weekend we went to the lake for swimming or shooting and hunting for goanna and kill and a cow and got leaves for the cow to turn the cow around then get the meat out from the cow and started cooking the meat. Then we went to put the meat in the trayback, then we went pick up people at the fishing place, then we saw a black-head snake. We miss it, the snake slide down the edge. We could not pull it so the snake went in the hole. We went back to the car and went to Mulan and started the cooking, the fishes eating.

Junior

On the weekend went to the lake and I cross over and got a swan egg. We cooked it just like normal egg and we went back to get more and it rained heavy. We slept in the car with a blanket; it was warm. All the way to Mulan. And I had a shower and I went to sleep. The next day we went to Two Tree and we cross over again, get more swan eggs. We got twenty of them and cooked them again and in the afternoon we had a little sleep and my mum and dad sneak off and I woke up my mum, and dad got a fright.

Junior Ovi

On the weekend we went to the lake for fishing and swimming, and then we went, someone left a fishing line behind. And then Luke saw the fishing line and Luke pulled the fishing line and he didn't know the fish was stuck and he pull it out of the water and he saw a big fish and got the fish and run with it and then we cook it up and we eat; it was delicious.

Samantha Togni
On the Edge of Two Deserts

I sat perched on a rock, watching the Easter moon rise above the pound and take its place amidst the pink and light blue hues on the horizon. I exhaled as my vision stretched out across the gentle creams, greens and reds of the endless plain beneath me. The pound, a natural amphitheatre, drops away from a plateau, and the exposed, deep red ridge of the plateau glows when the shadows are long. This is an ancient land that holds much knowledge and many stories. This pound was once part of an inland sea and the local Aboriginal people tell stories from the Tjukurrpa (Dreaming) of Luurnpa, the ancestral kingfisher, who created the waterholes and underground waterways in this country. To the uninformed there is little sign of water in this rock and spinifex country. This land holds its knowledge close; I am always a student in its presence.

I had watched the sunset at the pound countless times. It was always peaceful, providing solace and perspective at the end of busy, demanding days at the art centre. The sky was immense and the country seemingly infinite. It was a place where I felt on the edge of the world, or perhaps on the edge of my world. A threshold between sky and land, what is known and unknown, beauty and danger and between cultures. It was a place for me to think and attempt to bring some sense to the contradictions and challenges of my experience in this place.

This Good Friday moonrise, more than a decade ago now, was a moment to pause, take stock and gather our thoughts for the weekend ahead. Easter Saturday 2004 launched the *Balgo 4-04* event. More than twelve months in the planning and preparation, *Balgo 4-04* was an exhibition of artworks by artists from Warlayirti Artists, an Aboriginal-controlled art centre located in Balgo or Wirrimanu, a community on the edge of the Tanami and Great Sandy Deserts in Western Australia. The brainchild of my partner, who was the Art Centre manager, the *Balgo 4-04* event was developed collaboratively by the committee, artists and myself as the Warlayirti Artists director. It was part of the Art Centre establishing itself as a self-funding social enterprise, following its sudden de-funding as a result of its success.

The exhibition was the first of its kind in the eighteen-year history of Warlayirti Artists. It included more than one hundred works by forty or so artists that spanned the generations of artists painting at the time; works that had been collected for the show over the preceding eighteen months – they were the best of the best. And the exhibition was held not in a distant white-walled gallery, but in the Art Centre itself, hosted by the committee and artists, their families and the community in which many of them lived. A full-colour catalogue was produced and printed in Canberra, seven planes were chartered to fly in seventy visitors for the weekend, a team of seventeen volunteers was assembled from across the country to help, and materials were brought in to build new walls to hang the one hundred–plus works. All available accommodation in the community was booked but we accommodated the majority of visitors in tents, and sixty kilograms of kangaroo meat was ordered to make stew to feed the visitors and community, more than three hundred people. Were we crazy to be attempting this event in the middle of the desert? No, it was okay, the committee and artists were excited and producing amazing works for the show, collectors and art enthusiasts were eager and had secured their places to attend and with good planning and long hours, we were on top of the things that were within our control.

That just left Purkitji, Sturt Creek. Purkitji, to the north of Balgo, is part of the Lake Gregory catchment area. The creek crosses the Tanami Road, the main access road to the north, just to the south of the community of Kururrungku. The milky water, signalling that the creek would flood, had flowed down Purkitji a few months earlier. The closing of the road to the north had changed our plans for transporting some of our materials and supplies into Balgo for our event. We accessed these from Alice Springs along the Tanami Road to the south, instead.

However, as the days counted down to *Balgo 4-04,* Purkitji was still up and the road to the north remained impassable. This was a little concerning as there were some visitors who were planning to drive in from the north, but more importantly some of the key artists lived in Kururrungku and needed to be in Balgo for the opening. One of these was the celebrated artist Elizabeth Nyumi, who was included in the 2004 Biennale of Sydney. She had been on the telephone constantly in the weeks and days leading up to *Balgo 4-04* worrying about how she and some of her paintings for the exhibition would get there. A few days out from the opening, Nyumi rang announcing that she had a plan. She had arranged for the community's tin boat to transport her and her paintings across the milky water of Purkitji and requested that my partner drive to the southern side of the creek crossing to meet her the following day at a specified time. She was determined that Purkitji would not prevent her or her paintings from being part of this important event.

The rendezvous went like clockwork. Nyumi sitting in the tinny, framed by her large paintings being rowed across the flooded creek, as if a noble queen on her throne, was a sight to behold! It was an image that for me captured the importance, celebration and tenacity of *Balgo 4-04*. I took it as a sign from the ancestors and the gods that all would be well for our exhibition.

And so it was. The exhibition was ready, the paintings were hung, the galleries were gleaming, the catalogue had arrived, the committee was prepared for the opening, the kangaroo stew was made and the tents were erected. In the stillness of the early evening, we caught our breath watching that moonrise, nervously anticipating what the weekend would bring. A beautiful Balgo dawn welcomed Easter Saturday, as artists arrived early at the Art Centre to greet the visitors, and charter planes brought collectors, enthusiasts and supporters brimming with excitement and anticipation. The buzz outside the Art Centre was building as our volunteers made sure the visitors received their salads for lunch and their information packs. Following the opening speech, the artists and committee led the crowd into the gallery spaces and a cacophony of voices erupted as the power and presence of the paintings overwhelmed.

For several hours over that weekend, I sat at the sales desk constantly processing purchases and hearing stories of people's experiences. Smiles abounded, eyes were shining and the energy was infectious. Artists, their families, buyers and collectors mingled together and connected in a celebration of art, culture and people. The Easter Mass, highly regarded in the community, was held on the lawn outside Balgo's stone church on the Saturday evening. All visitors attended the mass, following the kangaroo stew supper they had shared with the artists and their families sitting on the verandah around the art centre.

On the Sunday afternoon, as the pilots did their final checks, the visitors piled into the back of the troopies for the short ride to the airstrip after saying their good-byes to the artists. Many who were leaving were in tears. Not only had they been captured by the art, they had been embraced by these people and affected by this experience in country. One visitor described the experience as an epiphany.

In the days that followed, the parish priest of seven years was talking to me about the weekend's event. He commented that as he walked along the Art Centre veranda on Easter Saturday, he had to look twice to recognise some of the people in the community he had known for many years. 'Their bodies were uplifted,' he said, 'they looked so proud and happy.' The experience of *Balgo 4-04* had moved people; both Aboriginal and non-Aboriginal.

Back out on the edge of the pound, more slumped than perched on a rock, watching the colours fade and the first stars appear, I realised *Balgo 4-04* was more than an exhibition; it was a rare occasion on which Aboriginal and non-Aboriginal people came together in a remote community, on the Aboriginal people's terms and invitation, to celebrate their art and culture, share knowledge and respect, and genuinely connect. It had exceeded expectations on many levels.

The Warlayirti Artists Committee had decided that part of the income generated through the *Balgo 4-04* exhibition would support trips back to country for the main artist family groups. Balgo was established as a Catholic mission in the 1930s and people came into the mission from the south as their traditional lands were taken over by pastoralists moving cattle through the country, spoiling waterholes and affecting traditional food sources. This means the traditional country that features in the artists' paintings is far to the south of Balgo and people rarely have the opportunity to visit the country that keeps their spirits strong and their painting alive. These trips back to country were an important outcome of *Balgo 4-04* that nourished the spirits and souls of the senior artists and their families. However, the outcomes of this event were many, some less tangible than others. A decade on, the legacy of the success of Balgo *4-04* lives on in many of us who participated; an extraordinary experience on the edge of two deserts, between two cultures, in which enduring friendships were forged.

Samantha Togni has worked with, and for, regional and remotely-based Aboriginal organisations in the areas of Aboriginal health, wellbeing, art and culture for the last 20 years.

Liz Poynton
Impressions of the Desert

Arriving by air after leaving the town of Broome – the turquoise sea meeting salt pans crossing long lines on the ground that seem to go on forever. Somehow those lines, dunes, rocks and white sand pan on till I arrive in Balgo hours later.

First thoughts: need a loo. The airport from the air had a few structures but alas, no loo. Ah well, behind the container will do…but what about snakes? I thought – quite irrelevant as the need was more urgent. But 'airport' indeed – more like 'air strip'.

Stepping off the plane…no tropical scents, just dry heat, quite overwhelming but not so overwhelming as the fact I am in the desert and it's all so big, red and dusty. Lots of new faces; things to learn.

Driving through town, I'm surprised at so many houses and people sitting outside, gathered amongst cats, dogs and children. Children were swimming and bathing in upturned fridges, with doors missing. Basic pools and looked like fun. Practical, I thought, 'recycled', but do they have fridges in their houses?

Going to the lake
New Year's Day: no clinic so a day off and able to leave clinic

unattended for a few hours with a note on the door, 'Ring Balgo'. Freedom to finally get to the lake. Finally, I say, as there had been previous attempts. Once with a doctor and nurse and me – once too early to the night and explored a path that led around the sand clay parts to the trees and into an enormous storm sky. The sky was darkening and looming towards us, clouds rolling and lightning striking. Initially we drove on till the realisation we weren't getting to the lake, didn't really know where the lake was and yes, we would maybe get very wet! The road could turn to mud and, well, yes, turn around and try another day. So next trip – four nurses and one who knew the way. We left Mulan by the right road past the old stockyards, past the dam where wild brumbies were drinking, past the barbed wire fence, only to realise once again we didn't know where the lake was. Sun was setting and we needed to turn around. Did I mention the lake is the size of Sydney Harbour? But still can't find it.

So, New Year's Day: sensible and finally arranged to go with some locals. Also learnt that you can't just go swim in their lake. The custom is that an elder has to 'mud' you so the serpent can't see you.

A bit of time and patience is needed in the desert. Arranged to meet at 9 a.m. but Caitlin assured us they wanted to go early, at 8 a.m., so the other nurse and I arrived at 8 a.m. sharp but Caitlin was not ready, so we came back a bit later (one year into the desert I no longer wear a watch). We had arranged to take five people to the lake. Eventually we closed the door to the troopie with twelve children and adults! I had brought a cake, oranges and water for five. Not being religious, we did a great job sharing, felt a bit like the loaves and fishes.

We left for the lake and enjoyed learning signposts on the way: the trees, the salt crossings, the car muffler, the dune and then…the one tree. We had arrived. Its vast, white-rimmed, aqua water; birds, swarms, brolgas, birds my father-in-law would know, magpie geese…he did teach me.

Travelling with locals I learn about their lake. Also they tell me stories and talk to me about who they are. 'Challenging' is a great word I have learnt to respond with when people ask about working in the desert. Most assume it has to do with dealing with the locals as compliance issues, teaching and communications with them may be challenging, but it's not. What is challenging is my belief in how the world works. It's challenging *me*: who I am, what I believe and why I think that way. That way it is Pandora's box. I actually have a house with a white picket fence; do I think everyone should live like that? Well, I never challenged that line before! Arriving in community it appears there are many houses but, on arrival, with my rose-coloured sunglasses on (they are rose trimmed) and I observe large houses. A few have trees; most have broken-down cars and lots of people sitting outside. The verandas are narrow so the locals make an area near a tree where dogs and children play. They sit and yarn. Sounds normal, but my house is designed with an outdoor entertainment area – shelter, table, chairs, barbeque area. I have seen a movie *Babakiueria* (Barbecue Area) made in the 1980s. I am not as naïve as I write: my brother was a lawyer who did land claims in the 1990s. This is not shocking my senses; it is challenging me materialistically and environmentally on what I take for granted that is not available to this community. Or is it? But are *things* necessary to the community members? I can't balance the influence of generations of hunter-gatherers and the mix, in recent times, of stockmen and missionary girls, and the 'imposed' community structures left behind.

There are not enough houses so families share, but the dynamics are always changing. Births and deaths rearrange who lives where. Visiting family members increase. Would more houses change or improve conditions? Yes, but the houses are a 'closed' design, not open to the elements that are harsh, understandably, but not open to communal living either. Not open to cooking outside in the fire, not open to a barbecue area, not open to family space or the people.

Middle of the day: houses are closed, air-conditioners on and the town appears ghost-like. It's human nature to conserve energy and stay out of the midday sun, but come early afternoon, as it starts to cool, the community comes alive. School finishes for the day, kids and dogs roam around. It's funny, we run the clinic from nine to four-thirty – we don't relate to the time of the people! We also should have a siesta at lunch and open later to accommodate the local time.

Challenges. I choose to live (now I say 'base myself') in Byron Bay, New South Wales – a microcosm of society. Federally we vote Labor; state, National/Liberal; and council, Green. So the town is an interesting collective, but most are environmentally aware, acknowledge social issues and accept progress based on maintaining land use and improving services to community and sustainability.

The challenge here, in the desert, is the local people's culture, and also us in maintaining or 'caretaking' their land. Somehow, the imbalance here is against environmental needs. Diesel generators for town electricity, solar hot water that is too hot most of the year and not functioning in winter when really needed. Recycling? Non-existent. Is it distance; is it just the wind or the dogs?

I couldn't believe my eyes as we drove closer to the town centre (shop) in Balgo. I am the generation of rubbish picker-uppers. Since moving to Byron and getting a canine friend, I even pick up dog poo! Is it a law? The council in Byron provides the bags at the dog beach. In Balgo I thought the rubbish truck must have exploded: wrappers, plastic bread bags, 'things' were everywhere. Driving towards the clinic I had to ask, 'What happened? How come there is so much rubbish everywhere?' My boss replied, 'White man's rubbish'.

Is this two hundred years of rubbish? The challenge began.

Family

One of the hardest parts starting in the community was family structure. Usually next of kin is mother/father, a yes or no answer. Tick the box and done. After a few months you realise aunty, grandmother, mother may actually be one and has nothing to do with giving birth. People nod their heads and think 'blood lines' for family tree but here you begin, and truly only begin, to understand family ties. Community ties, caring for one another, not a notion of ownership of individuals. A social worker suggested we should do a family tree as used by mental health in their assessments. Here it wouldn't be a tree but a jungle! And I don't know if one could ever complete it or how to make a diagram. Perhaps that is why, when they paint 'community', it is in concentric circles.

Names are also difficult. There is the challenge of how they are spelt or have been Anglicised because of mispronunciation, misinterpretation or how you assume it is spelt. Names change for skin names; if a family member 'passes' you can't say their name aloud, so if you share that same name it changes also. Luckily for the locals the nurses are all called 'Sister' so they know your name immediately. Years ago, when I worked on a Jackie Chan movie, he approached me and asked if I had been running that morning on the boardwalk as he thought he had seen me. 'Me? Run?' I replied, 'Not me'. He turned to the Hong Kong film crew and said something in Chinese to their amusement. Later I was told he said, 'You blondes all look the same to me!' Funnily enough, when I first started and went to the shops this would cross my mind. Locals would nod and you'd get a sense of belonging to the community, until someone comes to you and asks, 'Sister, you got any Panadol?' Then you realise you are the nurse and seen only as the nurse.

Having been in the community about a year now, there is a sense of connection as people nod, smile, 'click' to say hello – you know the noise out one side of your mouth, 'click'. It's so friendly to get a click! Truly! People recognise you – the nurses are Big Jeff – large and loveable; Yellow-Haired Girl, Beth – young, blonde and pale; and the Chinese One, who is Imee from the Philippines.

Kids

There is a cure-all injection we give when the kids have a sore throat or bad sores. My kids would never have had a penicillin injection for these illnesses. The rate of acute rheumatic heart disease is high in indigenous communities and prophylaxis is an important step in treatment for what seem minor symptoms. Unfortunately the indigenous die young with this heart disease so everyone knows it's time for injection if 'sick one'.

The kids like coming to visit the clinic: plenty of things to play with and might get an icy pole (Hydralyte) or even lollies (vitamin C tablets). If we are not busy it's great to see their faces. However, the faces become quite sad and worried if the visit to the clinic is for an injection. Early days – had the most beautiful, snotty-nosed girl of about three or four requiring treatment for school sores. She had one of those faces where the eyes draw you in and the white teeth jump out when the huge smile bursts out. So with a helper nurse and carer we gave the injections. Totally unexpected – wasn't the wriggling child, as the injection is painful, it was the colourful language, clearly spoken in English, 'You mother f—er!!' You know, I don't like injections either!

I have fallen in love. Yes, with the land, the sky, the lake, the vastness and the realisation of how small my footprints are on this land. But I have also fallen for a local. Since living here I have read about segregation and the separation of females and males. The difficulties of inter-racial relationships and that it was still illegal until 1975. So…yes. He is handsome and he is thoughtful. He is lean and you can feel the strength of his culture when we walk and he shows me tracks, animals, plants. Sadly, he is seven years old. But this is still a love story.

We met one afternoon when I was out walking with another nurse. Balgo has a point to walk out to see the sunset. Balgo Hills actually. Balgo is on top of hills of an area called a pound. The view is like one in a Western movie. There are Mezza's sparse trees, the lines of the road and no Coyote or Road Runners in sight. It's a great walk and of an afternoon Merle (nurse) and I had taken great pleasure in naming sites along the way and photographing things and sunsets.

So one afternoon a young boy on his bike tagged along. It

was unusual as he chatted while he rode beside us. He would stop to show us tracks – this is a camel track, this is a horse. I asked if he could do wiggles on his bike. He said no, but he could do snakes. Funny that I called them wiggles. I acknowledged he was right. We talked of family and his aunty is well known to us. She is a great artist; he is from a family of artists. The next time I returned from leave I brought him back crayons with Australian animals on each top piece. My thoughts were he might start drawing also.

Once again he joined our walking party and told me he had a secret, whispering, 'I am a drummer'. Well, so much for my crayons. He asked me to tell my friends his secret. Later we saw him at church. There's not much to do on a Saturday night and being a lapsed Catholic I go to church to show respect for the women who have such strong faith in a church that stole them. My friend suggested we come and see him play the drums. Opposite the church is an oval and basketball court with an undercover stage where the bands play, practise and entertain the community. There he was standing next to the drums with the 'swish stick', tap-tap-tapping to the beat. Yes…he was a drummer of sorts.

Next visit out I brought him back two sets of drumsticks. One has to be careful bringing presents so as not to shame people. It had been explained to me, so I went looking for my friend and found him near the shops. The sticks were in a package that I passed to him and he sped away home on his bike. You don't wait for 'thank you' as it will not come. He didn't expect a gift; he is humble. Unfortunately, I moved to another community and did not see him for some time.

Six months had passed since he told me his secret. It's Saturday night at church – he is in a blue shirt with a collar, hair slicked back and happy with the family around. He catches me up with his stories; he has a new dog, his uncle has a new baby and he is a drummer and will I come and see him play? Of course I will.

Walking home the following day we hear the band playing. You get to know the songs and the beat. I'm walking with two male nurses who comment that it sounds good. I ask if we can detour to see who is playing. They know I care about he who says he is a drummer!

As we approach the music is *really* good and we all start to realise, it's him, playing the drums, no adult, no swish stick but him keeping up with the band – his father plays guitar and sings. We are all excited and amazed. *He is a drummer; he is seven years old.* Later he wins the best new talent at the Battle of the Bands. His aunty told me; she knows it is something I would love to hear about my friend.

Billie, my dog, lives in Byron, and it was hard to leave her at home with friends. She is human and is loved by all. My friend, similar age to me, offered to mind Billie but she lives in an apartment and knows it wouldn't work. The offer came as she really felt Billie should have come to Balgo. On return after my first swing in Balgo, we discussed how much I miss dear Billie. My friend suggested I take her at least to try her in the community. When I explained we had 'camp dogs', she stopped me and asked, 'Are they gay dogs?', shrieking with laughter. I finally explained.

Helicopter

Helicopter is a master artist and has his own story. However, when he comes to clinic he chats about his art and tales. There is a Youtube clip of Balgo artists in Japan painting an Audi car.

I was discussing with Helicopter where he had travelled. He discussed Japan and Canada and said he had been to Melbourne and was going to Darwin. It's funny thinking this man from the desert is so well travelled. At this time I went to the pharmacy to get his medications. When I presented them to him he told me he had been to London and Europe.

As I child I had sung, repeatedly, 'Pussy cat, pussy cat, where have you been? I've been to London to visit the queen', so naturally I asked Helicopter if he saw the Queen in London. 'Yes', he replied, 'that lady has 'em a big house'. My mouth was wide open: people meet the Queen every day! What an extraordinary life he has led. My head was spinning with thoughts of what he had seen and accepted in his travels. It also made me realise one never knows how things really work – challenging again.

Earlier this year, my twenty-one-year-old son, Sam, asked me to travel to India with him. The dates slotted in my rotation and of course I was thrilled to be asked to go with him. Thinking he is not going to ask to travel with me often, I grabbed the opportunity. Hmm…'opportunity'. Why would a twenty-one-year-old want to travel with his mother? Obviously, I thought 'cos he loves me and we travel well together. Then I thought again – he has no money, he would like me to pay, he can stay in hotels if I go with him. Oh, the cynical mother. He had offered to pay for himself if we travelled on his budget level. Regardless of motive it was a yes, as any time spent with him is valued. Sam did an overland trip from Nepal to Delhi; my dates didn't quite fit so I spent a few days in India alone. We met in Mumbai, a city of twenty million people. That is Australia's population in one city! That is a long way from the Balgo population: six hundred (ish).

Travellers speak of 'culture shock' when exposed to new places or the enormity of change. Mumbai is a mass of people, pollution, noise, colour, scents; in Mumbai there are five million homeless. The contrast between wealth and poverty is overwhelming.

Sam suggested we stay at the Taj Hotel in Mumbai. This is the hotel that was bombed in 2008, and Lonely Planet and Sam believe for five-star luxury you can get a great deal. I remind you, Sam said he would pay for half. This is an opulent hotel looking at the Gateway to India where the boats would deliver the new arrivals. It is an oasis in a huge, overwhelming city. I realised whilst staying there that my shock wasn't due to the heat, the pollution, the extraordinary amount of security to enter the hotel (the Indian cricket team were also staying), the poverty, or the beggars, but the slow, creeping sensation of acknowledging that in Australia, my home, I was living in a third world country. 'Third world' is roughly defined as high infant mortality, low economic development, high levels of poverty, low utilisation of natural resources and heavy dependence on an industrialised nation. The nation is developing and less technologically advanced. The thought challenged me to the depth of my soul. How could this be, that I only thought this now I was in India? What blinkers did I have on back home in Australia? Social issues of grog, stolen generations, intervention, youth suicide, death in custody, diabetes added up to indigenous people's problems. Why didn't I think 'third world'? This was my culture shock, to recognise what was on my doorstep. In India people accept their social situation with 'it is God's way' or 'this is India'. Was I similar: 'this is Balgo'? Is this God's way? Do the locals accept their lot?

Spiritually aware in India, it resonated within me, the connection the locals have to the land and spirits of Dreaming. There are no statues of gods or flower offerings on every corner, but you can feel the enormous power from the sky, the land, and the lake. Do I recognise third world in Balgo, in the poverty? This is challenging, as there *are* houses, phones and iPads. It harps back to my white picket fence syndrome. Is this me being judgemental as I have many material objects and furniture? The locals don't have much furniture. Is it because it's not sold at the shop? Is it because it's too far away to deliver, is it because they don't want furniture, or need it, or it's broken, why bother?

I recognise their wealth of spirit, their faith in God and culture and family. I also recognise the dependence on industrial nations. Noel Pearson comes to mind: welfare and sit-down money? The dirge of society.

What did we take from the stolen generations? What did the missions do for these hunter-gatherers? What is Noel's radical hope?

Only some questions I have answers for, and even then it may be not what I want to hear or understand.

'This is Balgo.'

Liz Poynton works as a clinical nurse with KAMSC (Kimberley Aboriginal Medical Services Council).

Sheryl Anderson
A Limited Wardrobe

So, Balgo is great. The air is dry, and it has been mostly balmy. The first couple of weeks were both freezing and rainy, and I thought oh bugger, I have brought Maleny weather with me. We actually had the coldest May day on record (for Balgo). It was 13 degrees: freezing! And none of my stuff had arrived, so I only had a couple of items of clothing, no jumpers, no socks. I was wearing a couple of towels on my head and shoulders, and a blanket around my body!! Looked absolutely gorgeous. The Tanami Track got bogged and closed: all my gear was held up in Halls Creek until the road was declared open. Fun. Lucky my home, my little 'donga', has both air conditioning and heating. Heh.

Turned out, the guy who replaced the previous manager just up and left. Within two weeks of me arriving, he took off, and has been on sick leave ever since. Long story short: I haven't been able to do the actual art projects I came here to do. It is all a bit fraught, lots of challenges of the admin kind. A couple of years ago I vowed I would only do art. No more admin. Oh yowie.

I am trying to learn the language. Yowie is a great word, an exclamation of sympathy, empathy, commiseration, sorry sorry sorry.

Maybe a new Kukutja word a week is realistic when my brain is already full of the new (and ancient).

Please come and visit. It would be an experience you would never forget. If you could get yourself to Kununurra, I could pick you up. I was there on the weekend to collect our fly-in-fly-out bookkeeper. Left Balgo at 4 p.m., got a blow out (I was driving) in the dark on the Tanami Track. Tracey got up on the roof rack to get the spare tyre, and because it was too heavy to pass to me, dropped the tyre over the side, where it bounced away into the night. I had to chase the damn thing with only a very small torch. Lucky it only bounced and rolled for about fifty metres. Then had to roll it back through the sand, over the spinifex to the troopie.

We eventually got to Kunners about midnight, ready to drop our passenger – one of the local artists – off at her daughter's place. Turned out she couldn't remember where her daughter lived and kept giving directions that sent us around in circles. Ended up just parked, engine running, at a three-way intersection saying which way? Left or right or back the way we came? A car came up behind us, so I pulled off the road: it was the police. They wanted to know if we were lost; wanted my driver's licence; I had to be breathalysed and then they told us where the reserve was. So I drove there, still being told maybe left maybe right. M got out a couple of times to knock on the doors of houses she thought she knew (midnight remember) and then eventually told me that her daughter didn't have a house, but slept rough, under a bush!

'I'm sorry, we are not going to just drop you off in the middle of nowhere looking for a bush!', I said.

She came back and stayed with us for the night. Got to our rooms at 1.30 a.m. A very long drive!

I really love driving on the Tanami Track. Gravel, rocks,

sand, corrugations, lots of sand, potholes up the wahoo, and if you are driving at dusk (don't) there are also kangaroos, cattle, horses, bush turkeys. You have to keep your wits about you.

Anyhoo. I love my life at the moment. Having fun and adventures, but still miss you and the family and all my friends. Sal rings regularly, which is great. Someone to debrief to: it is quite stressful work. Got a couple of 'care' parcels in last week's mail plane. It was a welcome surprise to get a little card and tasty treats.

The mail plane is so important here: it only comes once a week, and someone from each workplace/agency is present, as well as many local people arriving in Balgo, and heading out. Quite a social event. You pick up your mail bag from the pile and give your outgoing mail (also in a big bag) to the pilot to send on. It is always exciting to get actual snail mail in that bag that is just for me, rather than business for the Art Centre.

Palya. Simple meaning: good.

Had a great week last week. Full but great. PAKAM (Pilbara and Kimberley Aboriginal Media) were in Balgo to do the Kapalulungu film, and with them was an anthropology student from the US, planning on doing his PhD on remote Aboriginal new media. He knows music and sound stuff. Some of the guys decided that they wanted to record a song for the background of the film, and so Wili got the sound studio going. About 100 people came in during the day, all wanting to record their songs. We couldn't get the sound actually playing back in the sound booth, or through the computer, so Wili just recorded on his small portable system.

I was trying to do paperwork in my office, but kept getting up to let people in and out of the cultural centre – there are still all the boomerangs and spears hanging around in there, and I have a responsibility to look after them. How weird is that. Anyway, Phil (the mental health dude) came in and asked if I needed an audio engineer, and if I did, I should ask the other film crew down near the airport.

Two film crews in a small community of 400 people. On the edges of the Tanami and Great Western Deserts.

Apparently there was another film crew in town. Of course. Documenting two ultralights flying from the South Australia coast across the centre to Broome, and filming peeps and community on the way. They also had six ground cars full of crew and a couple of indigenous guys from South Australia, one of whom was an amazing (ego-ful) muso and performer. They all turned up at the Art Centre with cameras. They got the sound going (well we all stayed late-ish and by 8 it was all working). Fantastic. So much fun. So much creativity. The place was alive and rocking.

la la la

Can't wait to start actually making some ART. Hope I get the chance to do my planned projects.

So, the day the ultralight film crew were in (they interviewed me) I was wearing an apricot shirt that I really don't like all that much. I feel very middle aged to old in it. I have worn it twice: the first time, the French film crew, documenting the worst roads in the world, arrived and interviewed me talking about Nora Wompi and Jimmy Tchooga paintings. The second time I wore it, another film crew arrived and filmed me chatting about Balgo art. Next time I wear that shirt, I am going to do my hair and put some make-up on!

A long low wailing. A sound I have never really heard before. It reaches into the gut and pulls. Pulls the tears up out of the centre of my heart to blur my eyes. I cry. I try not to sob. This old man is not my old man. But he told me stories. He was kind to me. And he was another link to a fading past. Is that right. Should I say that?

The wailing and occasional bursts of laughter from the kids continue. I wait in my office. Stop doing, start being as I hear the shuffling and the swishing leaves coming closer. A procession of grieving family and friends sweeps through the Art Centre, wailing and waving branches of gum trees over the floor, across the walls and down the doors. I am not sure what to do. I sit, my eyes cast down, my heart sad. One woman comes in and clasps my hands, then another. I am overwhelmed by a grief I do not really understand.

There are too many deaths here. Too many for such a small community. This man was much younger than my father. And my father isn't old. Not to me anyway. Most men who die here are too young. It isn't right.

We had to drive to Halls Creek to ask N, who is in respite there, to sign her three absolutely gorgeous prints. Planned to leave 1 p.m. Friday arvo. Ended up leaving 4 p.m. Driving straight into the sun, I hit a roo. First time. Awful. I was too short to see the road cos the sun was shining in my eyes, so Tracey took over. And then pulled over cos she felt something weird, maybe a flat tyre. Nothing. Then the car wouldn't start. So she hit the battery with a spanner. And it started. Then I was driving and the lights kept flickering, and the dashboard lights kept flickering, and the engine kept 'missing'. We were scared that the engine would just cut out and leave us coasting with no power, and no lights. So I drove slower than usual, particularly around the curves and hills. Took ages to get to Halls Creek. Quite stressful. A rum and coke fixed everything up. And a bit of a flirt with Philip at the bar. He knows the new priest at Balgo, and said he was going to visit us. Heh. I think he has an eye on Tracey. But I had my eye on him. Little bit of flirting.

And back at work.

Here's the thing. My grandmother died when she was eighty-five, and one of her last thoughts was of her first born – a baby, Kevin, who died when he was just eleven hours old. Over fifty years later, Ruby still grieved for her baby, still wondered just what went wrong, still asking questions.

She lived with that grief for most of her life.

I have a friend whose beautiful son was killed in a sporting accident; her grief is as profound now as it was four years ago.

I am now living in the desert in an Aboriginal community, working with people who find humour in nearly every situation, despite living on the poverty line, and despite the accumulated traumas that must have affected just how they are in the world.

I do not have children. I cannot begin to imagine how my grandmother, how my friend, really felt and feel at the loss of a child. But I have witnessed their feelings, I have seen how it affects their lives, how it changes every aspect of their life.

How then can the mothers and fathers, grandmothers, grandfathers, aunties and uncles, brothers and sisters cope and cope and continue to cope with all the trauma and stresses and grief upon grief that they have been subjected to, not only in the early days of the white settlement of this country, but every year since?

I cannot begin to imagine having my child taken from me, taken away to some unknown place for no understandable reason.

I cannot begin to imagine what it might be like for my child to commit suicide, as well as my nephew, and my young uncle, and my friend's son as well.

I cannot begin to imagine having to watch my sons and daughters lose themselves to petrol or alcohol or other dangerous substances.

I cannot begin to imagine having my child die because of the lack of good roads and good tyres.

I cannot begin to imagine knowing that the motika (motor car), so important to anyone living in remote Australia, might also be the cause of my son, my daughter, my partner going to jail because they haven't been able to pay their fines.

Oh yowie.

And I work with artists every day for whom this is the norm. They laugh and joke and create spectacular art, and tell me stories, of Tjurkurpa old and new, of bush tucker and where to go to find firewood. And are incredibly patient with me trying to understand, trying to learn. And laugh at my attempts at my Kukatja pronunciation. I am a visitor in this country.

Living in a remote community is hard for a kardiya, a stranger in their community. And I am a stranger. I am a stranger to their culture, to the seven languages spoken here, to their everyday way of life. Living here is…tricky. Many rewards. Lots of stresses. Lots of reasons to think 'why don't they…?'

And I remind myself of exactly where I am, and why I am here. And the context in which this community exists.

'Why don't I…?'

Last Saturday morning I was woken by a knock at my kitchen door. A couple from Melbourne wanted to visit the Art Centre, and also wanted to interview me and some artists for their magazine. So I quickly got dressed and raced over to let them in.

They started setting up a video camera on a tripod.

'Why the video?'

'Oh sorry, didn't I tell you, we have an online magazine.'

I was wearing that damn apricot shirt again. I don't like it, and because I don't like wearing it, it is often the only thing left clean in the cupboard.

No make-up. I told them the story of the previous three film crews and my shirt. He turned on the camera and started the interview.

'This is a spectacular Art Centre for such a remote place. But I understand you only have one shirt?'

La la la. No more.

Sheryl Anderson is Director/Manager of Balgo's Warlayirti Artists Aboriginal Corporation.

Pamela Brown
Life in Mulan

I come from a large family. I have five brothers and four sisters. My parents were born in the Caribbean on a small island called Grenada. They enjoyed fishing and living off the land but it was a hard life. In the 1950s they emigrated to the north of England. They suffered from a lot of racial prejudice but recognised the importance of dignity, self-awareness, family, community, and working hard to achieve.

My mum and dad understood the significance of a good education and always told me to go to school, learn what I can and try my very best. Dad often said, 'Education is your ticket out of poverty'.

Teaching in Mulan has been a real privilege. I love the dry, hot, sunny climate, the importance of family and community and the connectedness to the land and culture. Our school is committed to the concept of two-way learning, which respects and fosters the traditional Aboriginal languages of Walmajarri and Kukutja, and the culture of the people. Over the past two years I have learned that Aboriginal students bring a wealth of prior knowledge of culture, land, family and tradition to school. Relating to cultural experiences provides them with a sense of who they are. Literacy that works is based on content that is relevant to students and their everyday experiences. It is connected to their culture, tradition and spirituality.

All children love stories, listening to stories and telling stories. Mulan kids learn best through storytelling.

Jennifer
Telephone Reception in Mulan

Telephone reception in Mulan is quite unusual. Before heading out to Mulan we were told mobile service was non-existent, but that was not entirely true. On arrival the locals informed us we could get lucky sometimes and get one and half bars connected up on Telstra Hill. We'd seen small groups of mums with babies on hips, barefoot kids and teenagers making their way up and down there at sunset, assuming they were out for a walk. We thought the silhouettes we could see on top of the hill, facing east, were traditional owners glorifying some special spirit or god. Driving back into Balgo one day, we were close enough to see mobile phones raised in their hands, facing east as they all searched for the elusive connection.

Getting connected requires quite a bit of skill and patience – and there are no guarantees. A few of the quirky tricks that are highly recommended: move around on the top of that hill, left, right, back, forwards, cross the road, sit down, stand up again, stretch tall, stand on the bench seat, climb on top of the bench seat roof, sit on the purpose-placed wheel rim, sit in your troopie with the phone on the dashboard and when all else fails…go home and come back the next afternoon.

But never give up!

Tennant Creek, Northern Territory

Marie Munkara
Introduction

If anyone thought that Tennant Creek was just a boring mining town in the middle of nowhere full of boring people with boring lives then they should think again. The Desert Stories workshops proved that the place is buzzing with amazing literary talents that were just waiting for an opportunity to burst forth and shine like stars in the desert.

The workshops attracted an interesting cross-section of literati including high school students, firemen, police, public servants, arty vegetarians, bountiful bloggers and more. Poetry and prose flowed like a bottle of exceptional wine. Each workshop was packed with interesting, and at times sensational, interaction from workshop participants who continued to inspire each other and, I might add, myself as well. The peals of laughter in the tea room at the Ali Curung Art Centre might have raised an eyebrow or two but none of us cared as the stories came thick and fast. What a great place.

The number of participants in each workshop varied between three and six. This provided great opportunities to get to know them personally and to talk about the directions they wanted to take with their writing. It was good to see the initial reluctance of a few to disclose their real love of writing give way to passionate discussions about what was really going on inside. 'I only write brochures', said one lady, only to admit later that she loves writing poetry. The moving poetry of one young man whose work involves working with those whose lives are full of turmoil and destruction was indescribably touching. And with the UFO capital of Australia just 100 km south of Tennant Creek at Wauchope it was just brilliant to have some cleverly crafted science fiction to add to the mix. Lyrical descriptions of the desert and stories about family and self were as engaging and funny as they were heart wrenchingly sad.

In addition to the workshops were individual meetings with people who couldn't make it because of work commitments or personal reasons. These were held in cafés, supermarket aisles, and petrol stations, over fuel bowsers and on the phone. The community of Tennant Creek was extremely supportive and I was approached on a number of occasions by people who knew I was in town and just wanted to wish me well.

In total I met with twenty-nine people either in the workshops or individually, at the women's shelter, Barkly Arts, the high school and the Anyinginyi Congress.

In conclusion I need to thank my amazing assistant Ktima Heathcote who arranged times, places, people and food. It wouldn't have been the same without her. I worked with the participants, who are contributors to the anthology, and some work had to be done but not much, a reflection of the high quality of works submitted. Overall I believe the contribution from the Northern Territory to the *Desert Writing* anthology to be truly noteworthy. The writers of Tennant Creek are an amazing bunch and I was blessed to have worked with them. The scenery was pretty damned spectacular as well.

Of Rembarranga, Tiwi and Chinese descent Marie Munkara was delivered on the banks of the Mainoru River in Arnhemland by her two grandmothers and spent her early years on Bathurst Island. Her first Novel "Every Secret Thing" (UQP) won the David Unaipon Award in 2008 and the NT Book of the Year in 2010. She has published two children's books *Rusty Brown* and *Rusty and Jojo* (Laguna Bay Oxford Press, 2014) and her second novel *A Most Peculiar Act* (Magabala, 2014). Marie has recently completed her memoir (Penguin / Random House) and is currently working on a TV mini-series.

Ktima Heathcote
Introduction

I count myself lucky to live in the desert. Ever since my birth in Wittenoom, a now defunct asbestos mining town in the Pilbara region of Western Australia, I have been inexorably drawn like a magnet to red dirt and big blue skies. I have lived in cities for most of my life – Perth, Brisbane, Sydney and London to name a few. But the call to the wild, to places where rocks dwarf people, clouds are tinted with dusky pink and bushes bathe in soft copper light, sat unrequited in my belly. Then fate or foolhardiness, call it what you will, sent me packing to the Northern Territory more than six years ago to live and work in another former mining town.

Tennant Creek sits on Warumungu land. It is part of a region called the Barkly, a huge expanse of around 320,000 square kilometres with a strong Aboriginal culture, a cattle industry and a gold mining history. The area is awash with stories and storytellers. Locals throughout the region have a distinct desert creativity and humour, too. You need one when it's a 234 kilometre round trip over rough, unsealed roads just to attend a poetry master class in town.

I came across my first group of writers in October 2009, three months after arriving in this dusty town. I'd landed the job of organising a writers' retreat for Barkly Regional Arts, a not-for-profit arts resource and networking organisation tucked away in a classroom-sized office in a low-set complex of buildings a few blocks back from the Stuart Highway. This is the pulse, the heartbeat, of the local arts scene, where out-of-towners descend when they want to discover what's going on.

The writers I met were a diverse bunch – Aboriginal and non-Aboriginal, some published, others who were somewhat fresh to the world of writing, storytellers and poets as well. For a week we took part in workshops facilitated by visiting Brisbane poet Yvette Holt. It was a rare opportunity to listen to the language of two different cultures. The Aboriginal writers mainly wrote about the land, their country, as so evocatively expressed by Maureen O'Keefe, a writer from Ali Curung, a community about 170 kilometres south of Tennant. Unconstrained by the straitjacket of 'correct English', there's a natural rhythm in the way Aboriginal writers out here express themselves. Like the surrounding countryside, harsh and uncompromising during drought, green after rain, their voices seep into your skin and ignite an ancient, almost forgotten part of yourself.

The non-Aboriginal writers of the group showed more structural complexity in their work. They focused more on feelings and how they see themselves in relation to the world. It's an avenue not commonly explored by Aboriginal writers out here, but excavating memories and personal experience for their rich emotional content is starting to fuel the work of established writers.

Having a well-planned and inclusive writing retreat in an area often overlooked by funding bodies created a kernel of hope for the literary minds of this region. Less than a year

later, in July 2010, Barkly Writers' Ink was born. With the aid
of an Arts NT community grant of $5,000, a core group of
writers from the Barkly was able to meet on a regular basis to
write, provide support and professional development, network,
mentor each other, and learn about the craft of writing and the
publishing industry.

I was the birth mother – or the newcomer in the right
place at the right time – and for the next three years organised
workshops, arranged opportunities for public readings, applied
for more grants, drove writers to literary festivals in Darwin
and Alice Springs, handed out encouragement and cups of tea
in equal measure and established long-lasting networks with
the NT Writers' Centre and published authors such as Marie
Munkara.

When Marie approached me in September 2013 about
packing up her car with papers, pens and ideas and driving
down to the Barkly to meet up with local writers for a project
called Desert Writers, I jumped at the chance. Workshops were
arranged and big open spaces provided inspiration once again
as wordsmiths walked across country, inhaled desert dust or
admired the night sky with stars as bright as diamonds. Set
against the palette of ochre reds and yellows, Tennant Creek
and the Barkly region are known as the Golden Heart of the
Northern Territory. The hours spent with Marie brainstorming
and writing reminded all ten participants, seven of whom are
published in this anthology, once again of the proximity of heart
to beauty, of language to landscape.

I am grateful for the opportunity to be mentored by
someone of the calibre of Marie, as are my fellow writers –
Adrian McNamara, Jon Hodgetts, Maureen O'Keefe, Matthew

McKinlay, David Curtis and Rosemary Plummer. We were all fortunate to have her support and her gentle praise.

There is great literary potential here in the Barkly and in the group published in this anthology, of that I have no doubt. Maureen won a scholarship in 2014 to receive mentoring from Magabala Books, an indigenous publisher in Broome, WA. Matthew has his own poetry blog and has been known to let his inner wolf roam the performer's stage. Award-winner Rosemary has a long list of publications to her name. Adrian, David and Jon share a unique experimental voice and show real promise. As for myself, I love to drink in the desert light at dusk and be serenaded by the chatter of white cockatoos settling on branches for the night. I try to explore where I live as a way of being as much as of capturing a sense of place. I love mystery. I love murder mysteries. I love this land. I am enriched by its language. And so my story for this anthology, as much as my own story, has been carved out of country and its mysterious pull on my psyche.

Here, the wellspring of creativity is as deep and as limitless as the red sandy country that stretches into infinity. The land and its inhabitants are also raw and extreme. Complexity greets me every day on every street corner of this dusty town. I've tried to leave countless times. As Paul Simon's song goes, 'there must be fifty ways to leave your lover'. There are, I've discovered, as many reasons to stay. One day while sipping a cappuccino at a café in the main street of Katoomba, I contemplated life in this Blue Mountains town. 'Kateemia, you come home now', a voice said in my head. It belonged to an Aboriginal musician from Tennant. A few days later I flew back. I can't explain why.

In time I will leave. My heart will grieve. Like spinifex tips stinging my skin, there is no way out when in the thick of it but through. Even so the softer animal part of me will remember, always. My bones rattle with the sound of black storms gathering on the horizon. Dust devils are ingrained in my feet. My skull has been branded by the sun. Wind has caressed the backs of my hands. At other times it has torn through my body, ripping away the structures of a Western upbringing as easily as a cyclone peels off a tin roof.

I am a desert writer for life – even if one day I sit by my other home, the sea. My throat is infused by intense blue, gun metal greys and greens of varying hues. My lips curve in joy at the blossoming of a delicate desert rose. I carry a canvas of clouds in my eyes. I am as rooted in this land as a gnarly mulga tree.

Ktima Heathcote is an emerging writer living in Tennant Creek. She coordinates Barkly Writers' Ink and is having fun writing poems and short stories inspired by the dusty red landscape she now inhabits. A tabloid journalist by trade, Ktima has had a few non-fiction essays published including on the work of local Aboriginal artist Dion Beasley (Primavera, 2012) and an article about the local writing scene in Tennant (*Meanjin*, Melbourne, v.70, no.3, Spring 2011: 13-16). In August 2015, she was awarded a Writer's Residency by NT Writers' Centre in Eco House, Botanical Gardens, Darwin. Ktima tries, unsuccessfully at times, to juggle writing with full-time work. She doesn't know how she found the time to write, let alone finish, *The Cooper Chronicles*. But she's determined to find a solution. An Australian by birth, she's currently obsessed with her years living in England.

Rosemary Plummer
Tough and Rough

Out in the desert very little to be known.

My dad Teddy Plummer was a mighty man, tall and strong.

He grew up rough, tough, without having any education in the rugged bush prickle land of the Barkly.

He was a stockman droving, droving cattle from Phillip Creek Northern Territory to Camooweal in Queensland. Years passed, the cattle industry was taken over by road trains and there were no jobs left. Skilled, experienced and having his culture and knowledge he learnt white man's trade. How to be a plumber fixing toilets and broken pipes at Warrabri government settlement. That's where Teddy got his surname Plummer, from working as a plumber.

This story happened many years ago between the 1950s and 60s.

Dad learnt to speak English from working and having non-Indigenous friends. Significantly he helped a researcher by the name of Prithrinda Chakravarti in 1966 with the Warumungu language. He had been told by the Australian government to do the Waramungu language urgently because the government must have thought it was one of the dying languages at that time. Later Prithrinda became a lecturer during the 1990s at

Batchelor Institute of Indigenous Tertiary Education (BIITE). By chance he told me about my dad and that he was a very good storyteller among Warumungu people.

My mother May was a loving person and loved going to church on Sundays, singing Christian songs praising the Lord. We too as children loved singing. She dressed seven of us, five boys and two girls, properly making sure the clothes were good. She cared with a gentle warm heart and wanted us children to get somewhere and to have a job in the future. She was a wonderful wife to my dad and she cooked food three times a day and made sure that everybody ate. Sometimes she cooked cake. She even sewed clothes like dresses and trousers and ironed the clothes on the old wood stove. She scraped the floors with a scraping brush. She too was a clever lady. Unfortunately mum died tragically in the early 70s at the age of thirty-two. Dad had to raise the seven of us with the help of his parents and other family.

Every Saturday night dad used to put on his wireless, broadcasting live around Queensland and parts of the Northern Territory from Mount Isa, and listen to the Ranch Club. People requested their favourite country music like Slim Dusty, an Australian recording artist, and others like Johnny Cash, Buck Owens, Skeeter Davis and Patsy Cline from America.

Dad had a passion for football and dearly loved Warrabri, now Ali-Curung, footy team. Whenever the men came into Tennant Creek to compete against others in the Barkly Football League, he barracked for Ali-Curung even though he had grandsons playing for Tennant Creek Eagles.

As a leader he faced a lot of racism, not just from the whites but with his people calling him names and saying, 'Ah, he thinks he's white'. From the white perspective they called him coon. One day at Renner Springs the shopkeeper did not serve him food. That did not worry him or make him bitter or angry. He took it and said, 'It okay, alright'. He was humble, not aggressive, but did his best for children and the people.

He loved going hunting, shooting kangaroos, emus, bush turkeys and goannas. With the Land Rover he was a good and skillful hunter. One day he did not have bullets left to shoot a turkey, but he had the bush skill to creep up and hit the turkey on the head. That was the meal for the evening.

Several years later when he was in a nursing home he received a letter from an old superintendent, Bill Cobar. Bill said in the letter: 'Remember the night we stopped a fight between two tribes Walppiri and Alyawarra and both stood on the opposite side of the oval in the middle of the night with boomerangs, nulla nullas, arguing about a cowboy movie that was shown that night. One man said to another "oh that's me because I am wearing cowboy shirt and trousers".' That story made dad sad and he cried and said, 'Oh gee, oh gee'. According to Bill in that letter 'there were no Police Station or Policemen back then'.

Dad had a stroke a few years later. After mum died he managed to live on until the age of eighty-three. Whilst at Ali-Curung (formally Warrabri) he was awarded a British Empire Medal (BEM) from the Queen for community work and as a mediator between different tribes and non-indigenous people.

Rosemary Plummer is a Warumungu woman from Tennant Creek. She was born at Phillip Creek Mission during the movement of Aboriginal people from their country to another language group's land in 1955 and the government took children away from their mothers. A traditional owner of this area, Rosemary currently works for Catholic Care NT. She is a mother of three, an auntie, grandmother and great grandmother of two.

Rosemary started writing in 1992 after a discussion of the Coniston Massacre of 1928 and the movement of Aboriginals from their homelands, and the change from traditional ways of living. After all these talks she broke down and out of this grief she wrote her first poem, *Tribal Women*. This poem first appeared in *Voices from the Heart*, an anthology of Aboriginal poetry. Since then Rosemary has had work published in various collections around Australia.

Jon Hodgett
Storm in a Ti Cup

If you're not an Australian and especially if you've never visited, images of the country you may conjure up might include the red earth, kangaroos, maybe a vast cattle station, indigenous Australians, fellas drinking stubbies of XXXX with a cowboy booted foot resting upon a rail. However, most of inhabited Australia is an urban metropolis awash with fast food outlets, traffic, office workers. There are beaches with their surfers but mostly the similarities with other Western cities are more apparent than the differences. Indeed, Melbourne has created one of the finest coffee cultures in the world and we, as Australian residents, are becoming quite the needy children tugging on the apron strings of our baristas. Living in the outback, as I do, does not seem to have quashed our want for a Melbourne cuppa.

Tennant Creek, my home for two years, reflects that imagery of our imaginations. The Golden Heart of the Territory, it is a town with a population of around 3,000. Its nearest neighbour, our regional centre, is Alice Springs just 505 kilometres south. The Alice, as it's known locally, is the third-largest town in the Northern Territory after the capital, Darwin, and a Darwin suburb once distinct, Palmerston. Ten per cent of Territorians live in Alice Springs, which is a whopping 25,000 people. To get to the next biggest town you'd have to travel 1,500 kms back north to Darwin/Palmerston or the same south to Adelaide. Don't even try and go in any other direction since you'd run out of bitumen pretty quickly and food and water shortly after. But for us outbackers, a town of this size is an urban nirvana. There might not be the ocean or surfers but there are fast food outlets, there are office workers, maybe not traffic, but there is more than one set of traffic lights and multiple roundabouts too. There's a shopping centre, a car wash, a sports clubs, a reptile park. You can eat at dozens of restaurants, drink in a variety of bars, and have a proper coffee made by a real barista in a café that wouldn't actually look out of place in Melbourne. However, I'm going to talk about a stop en route from Tennant to Alice, the only stop where one can purchase a coffee without putting a token in a machine.

The journey south to Alice from Tennant Creek takes in one largely straight road, and by outback standards is relatively short, coming in at under four and a half hours. With Northern Territory speed limits at a generous 130 kilometres per hour, the ute's cruise control does the bulk of the work. The landscape is mostly flat, with the red soil dominated by grasses and low, scraggly shrubs. With the inevitable clear blue skies above, the reds, greens and yellows of our roadside seem sharp. After 80 kilometres of travelling south the road begins to weave through low rises and then Karlu Karlu appears, or the Devil's Marbles, a collection of oversized boulders perched perilously upon craggy rock formations. An incredibly popular spot during the cooler winter months with the grey nomads, the caravanning retirees who crawl up and down the arterial Stuart Highway, which ultimately runs from Adelaide on the South Australian coast to Darwin on the Northern Territory's, Karlu Karlu contains many spots sacred to the various indigenous language groups that once lived their semi-nomadic lifestyles around the region, with this spot being a neutral meeting place. Now, the only meetings are those around a camp fire as the nomads share a bottle of shiraz outside their luxury motor homes and goose-necked caravans.

Just south again is the first of three roadhouses before reaching the only town between Tennant Creek and Alice Springs, Ti Tree. 'Town' is a bit of a loose definition; it's more of a community that is on the highway. 'Community' is the term given to Aboriginal population centres, and their size, which can vary anywhere from tens of inhabitants to a thousand, will dictate what services exist. For most, these may include a medical centre, visited on a roster basis by health professionals, maybe a small school, a football field, even a shop. Those that reside on the highway, such as Ti Tree or Elliott, 250 kilometres to the north of Tennant Creek, might have a pub, a roadhouse, a police station, maybe even employment opportunities. Ti Tree has all of them for its population of around 150, but also for the cattle stations and other regional communities nearby, which swell the population to nearer 1,000, as well as those passing through. For me, it's my coffee stop and a time to stretch the legs, since they've not touched a pedal since leaving Tennant Creek. Even my hands have barely had to move from the 'ten to two' position on the wheel. I say 'coffee' but really that's an affront to baristas the world over who would not recognise what I'm drinking as anything other than a turgid, too hot, too milky, distinctly not coffee-flavoured cup of bile. Of course, this does not stop me from having one every time I pass through. I think my relationship with outback coffee is akin to Stockholm syndrome.

Ti Tree offers not only a roadhouse, a place for fuel, beer and counter meals, but also a general store, home to my hot beverages. The store is a hundred yards or so down a dirt track and though not much of a diversion, it took me two Ti Tree stops to make the most of it. Before this, the roadhouse that sits conveniently in the middle of the town was just a casual braking and gentle steer to the left that provided my caffeinated beverages. Or actually, it didn't. The first time the machine had broken, which is forgivable. When things go wrong out here, they can takes weeks to fix. A Mac-owning friend had to wait two weeks for his computer to be repaired because the IT guy in town only does PCs, so off to Alice Springs the Mac went, and then a spare part needed to be sent on the three-hour plane journey from one of the major cities and then get fitted, and, well, you can see my point. The second time at the roadhouse though really got my goat.

Coffee here doesn't really come in variations. A flat white is the same as a latte and both are the same as a cappuccino, except the cappuccino has chocolate sprinkles dusted over the top of it at the end. People are buying these fancy machines but no-one actually knows how to use them. So I ordered a regular coffee. Instead of speaking to me, the grumpy old man behind the counter just pointed at a sign above my eye-line on top of the bain marie away to my right. 'We are not mindreaders', it said. 'Flat White, Latte, Cappuccino', it went on. 'Ah, sorry, I'll have a flat white please'. More pointing whilst I read on down 'small, medium, large'. 'Um, the medium one then'. Still the pointing continued, his frown deepening, and I was beginning to feel a little unnerved. I was also struggling since I was fairly certain I'd just ordered a medium flat white. I quickly scanned the sign again. He was still pointing. Type, check. Size, check. Eventually, he tersely broke the silence. 'Sugar?'. 'Ah, no, no thanks'. There it was, right at the bottom of the sign, 'sugar?' The sign was right, they are not mind-readers, but I'm comfortable in ordering a regular coffee and expecting an individual facing a customer to interpret that information and make me a medium flat white without sugar or, as it used to be known, a regular coffee. There were even sugar sachets right in front of me. If I had a late change of heart and desperately craved a saccharine addition, I was secure in my ability to add it myself. Our exchange lasted far longer than even a quick 'Do you mean medium and would you like sugar in that?' We had silence, staring, pointing and glaring. I've never handed money over with so much malice and ill-feeling, and snatching my coffee, I marched out of that roadhouse vowing never to return. Slammed the door of my ute as I settled in to continue the drive, took my first sip of the drink and burned my tongue. No, that was the last time I went to the roadhouse. Now the store gets my trade except it's only open six days a week and doesn't tell you which one it's closed on but it is open 8 a.m. to 5 p.m., except for the day I drove to Alice Springs in the morning, collecting my cuppa at 8.05 a.m., and then back through at 3 p.m. to find it shut. I'll forgive them all that because the coffee is better (a relative term) and they're nice in there, but let me assure you, Melbourne this ain't!

Jon Hodgetts moved to Tennant Creek in early 2012, although left for Alice Springs in 2014, to take a job with the regional pastoral landcare group, Barkly Landcare and Conservation Association. This took him all over the Barkly visiting and working on some of Australia's largest and most iconic cattle stations. The comfort with which he adapted to the remoteness of the region inspired Jon to write about some of his experiences with a newly found Outback outlook. Jon now keeps a blog as a result of this anthology.

Matt McKinlay
Drug of Choice

Drug of choice
Dull the pain
Ease the ache of depression's reign

Drug of choice
Which will it be?
One that is the master of hungers' key

Drug of choice
When life gets too real
Will a crystal let me have the chance to feel?

Drug of choice
When the workday is done
The only way I can unwind and have some fun

Drug of choice
Used to take the pain away
Now it seems I'm in pain every single day

Drug of choice
When my inspiration can't get through
One whiff and my mind takes an alternative view

Drug of choice
With a life full of hardship and pain
Can I go on without comfort shot straight in a vein?

Drug of choice
So many out there, one for every ill
Dance the black spiral just by dropping a pill

Drug of choice
Now even sugar and caffeine
Fight to rule my life, turn it into something obscene

Drug of choice
Time to change, seize the day from drugs' control of me
Time for lucid dreaming and at last be free

Long Way Back

Long way back
New roads past the burning bridges

Paths less travelled
New beginnings struck with every step

Recriminations and scorn
With every glance and half hearted conversation

Road so long
Dark clouds hover over past horizon, spread discord
over new promise

Keep carrying on
Tainted by doubt, resolved in love's embrace,
reborn in firm direction

Long way back
Each new deed forged of newfound desire

Dreams reshaped, transformed
Heart, mind and soul conjoined with the will and
determination of another

Redemption salvation determination
Bring a voice to those found mute, direction to those
found lost

Passion honour duty
In all things lest they fade, to bring some measure of just
ending to loss, hurt and anger

Stand tall, strong
Enthusiasm, boundless, infectious, undaunted by any setback

Shining new horizon
With both hands held strong, firm in belief and courage, with
a will to carry on.

This Town

Like gemstones glittering in the night
The steady glow of streetlights
The wake of past nights' shame

For every bottle thrown down in anger
A shattered life, a broken dream
The golden heart of the Territory
More tarnished with each scream

With the dawn, the light of day
Community renewed
To find each nightly discord
Is not the many, but the few

Though travellers mistake one street
Call it the essence of the town
Drive through with fearful hearts, windows up
and doors secured
No chance illusion will be revealed

Worse still to warn off others
From discovery revealed
A depth of culture, spirit and resolve

The mark of community close knit
There lies the heart that shines as gold
The many that band together
Balm the spirit of the town

Give comfort and meaning
To lives under constant shroud

Though appears a grave injustice
For all who stand their ground
Refuse to let slight and insult
Dim the flame of hope, inspiration, potential

Veins filled with golden dignity
Flowing through each and every one
All people taking breath as one strong land
People of the mulga curtain
Drawn wide to show the light.

Matthew McKinlay was born in Melbourne and raised in Townsville. He spent several years with the Australian Army in Darwin and ended up spending seven months in East Timor. After that, he changed uniforms to the local police and has been there ever since. He has been working in Tennant Creek for the past three years, as a Youth Diversion officer and more recently as a Domestic Violence officer. Writing comes as a hobby, as does stand-up comedy. Matthew is a frequent contributor to ABC Open online and ever hopeful of future printed writing success.

Ktima Heathcote
The Cooper Chronicles – Featherfoot

Sergeant Cooper thought it was a dead animal at first. The frenetic movement of his windscreen wipers batting at the driving rain and the build-up of steam inside his car made it hard to see. But as Cooper slowed down he made out the shape of two humans. A boy and a girl were huddled down on the side of the road, a grey army blanket wrapped round their shoulders. He eased his car over, making sure not to skid on the loose red gravel. The boy and the girl stood up, threw off the sodden blanket and jumped into the passenger seat before Cooper even had time to stop.

The girl sat on the boy's lap. He pulled out a comb, slim and metallic, from the back trouser pocket of his black stovepipe jeans and started raking it through her long, red hair, droplets of rain glistening in the gloom of the car. They looked no more than seventeen.

'What are you kids doing out here at this time of night?' Cooper asked.

'Car broke down', said the girl.

'We were going to walk to the nearest town, but it started to rain.'

'You should never leave your car, you know.' Cooper was about to admonish them with a wag of his finger, but thought better of it. 'Not out here, not in the desert, even at night. There's no-one around.'

'Well, we met you, didn't we?' said the boy.

This was the first time he'd spoken and Cooper detected a sneer.

'Sure', said Cooper, twiddling knobs on the radio in the vain search for a station. 'Anyways, the nearest town is Warrego Springs, 'bout 100 kilometres down the road. I'm heading that way, so youse can get a feed and a good night's rest. There's a local mechanic, goes by the name of Tommy. He'll head out to your car in the morning, no worries. It'll cost you – a carton of Gold stubbies that is.'

'No!' said the girl.

Cooper flinched at the violence of her outburst. The night and the constant rain were already wearing on him and now these two kids.

Sensing Cooper was tiring of them, the girl mumbled an apology. She lowered her lashes, thick and long like spider's legs, then raised them a touch to fix her pale green eyes on to Cooper. She was pretty enough, pale skin, long, wavy hair and a petite, upturned nose. Cooper simply wasn't in the mood. He let his mind linger on the cute nurse he met at the RSL the previous week though, especially her sweet lips and soft black curls. She was thirty. She was not a kid.

'We know this might sound crazy but we've, well, we've been discussing our options and we'd like to go back to our car,' said the girl. 'It's not far.'

Cooper rubbed his eyes and squinted through the windscreen as sheets of rain bounced off the bonnet. He didn't remember them talking to each other.

'We gotta get to Alice Springs for a mate's wedding. If we stay another night, we won't get there in time. We've only got a flat tyre...' The girl's voice trailed off.

'You can fix a flat, can't you Mr Policeman?'

There it was again, unmistakable this time, a sneer, as if the boy, with his empty sky-blue eyes, were questioning his manliness, goading him to take a wrong turn.

'Sure', answered Cooper.

Cooper was driving his Valiant that night. He'd left the patrol car at home, so he could visit some of his mob out bush. But the navy blue uniform, creased and stained with sweat from sitting for too long in a hot vehicle, and police cap on the back seat offered more than enough clues for the two passengers.

The girl turned to the boy and frowned. The boy simply shrugged, folding plump, childlike lips into a smirk. His hair was dark, lank. His skin was unnaturally pale. His ears were pierced, the lobes stretched by round black plugs. He wore the uniform of small town youth – tight T-shirt, skinny jeans and scuffed black desert boots.

Turning back to Cooper, the girl lowered her lashes again, deliberately leaning her head sideways and slowly brushing her hair behind her neck and shoulders, exposing milky white flesh. Her wet cotton dress, like a second skin, hid little.

Cooper's eyes gave nothing away either as he reached for the dash, his fingers scrambling over grit, tissues, an assortment of feathers, tattered and faded from lying in the sun, a half-finished chip packet and an empty can of Coke to find his water bottle.

'One of youse get in the back?' Cooper said, his irritability rising with each swig of warm water. 'And put your seatbelts on.'

Taking his foot off the accelerator, Cooper tapped the brakes gently and shifted down a gear ready to pull over but the girl had already moved. She squeezed herself through the gap between the two front seats, the material of her thin dress fluttering over Cooper's arm, and settled herself behind the boy.

Cooper shifted uncomfortably.

She curled a forefinger to stare at a nail. From a plastic bag she pulled out a file, thin and metallic like the boy's comb. The skin around her fingernails was raw and red.

'We were driving a hire van. They're called Wicked. You know the ones?'

Cooper did. He didn't bother to reply. He drove on. Only two weeks ago three Swedish backpackers rolled one of those vans after driving too fast through floodwaters. No one was seriously hurt. Lucky. Not everyone is. Cooper was over the foolishness of tourists.

In the past stupidity suited him. He used it to his advantage, especially as an ambitious, young police constable in Adelaide trying to outsmart the dope dealers, pimps and petty thieves. But not now, not since a foolhardy decision led to his mate's murder and not since reconnecting with the old man, his Uncle.

Cooper's memories of Uncle, a powerful medicine man, were as fresh as the smell of rain as he drove on and on into the silent night, his two passengers lost in their own crazed thoughts.

Uncle wore slippers woven of emu and cockatoo feathers, matted with human hair and blood. Cooper saw them once in a wooden box at the foot of the old man's lumpy, filthy mattress. They were sitting on top of kangaroo skin, ready to be wrapped. Cooper reckoned he was about twelve.

'Don't touch them or you'll die', Uncle warned. Cooper

winced at the idea of so much power, of being so close to a Kurdaitcha man. With a quick pluck of a strand of human hair Uncle could be paid to kill, cripple or curse someone. As a kid Cooper saw half the town of Warrego Springs, even the white priest from the Catholic Church, cross the street when that old man approached.

When Cooper had returned to Warrego Spring several months earlier he didn't get the welcome home he'd hoped for. He was the nephew of a featherfoot and many of his mob were wary.

It was the girl's voice, sweet and high like a child's, that brought Cooper abruptly back to his vinyl seat, now sticky with sweat.

'We don't wanna leave the van. All our stuff is there and we don't want someone nicking it.'

Cooper ignored her and stared out the windscreen. It was still raining, hard and sharp as needles, and he could barely make out the outline of scrub, dark against a backdrop of watery grey.

A bolt of jagged light hit a ghost gum on the roadside, lighting up the car interior like a Christmas tree and casting the faces of Cooper and his two passengers half in shadow. The air con had long since packed in.

'No one with any sense would be out in this shit', Cooper mumbled, mainly to himself.

'We really wanna go back to our van', said the girl. She was whining now.

Cooper half turned to the boy, keeping one eye on the girl through the rearview mirror.

'Not gonna happen', he said, gradually easing the Valiant off the roadside to pull into a rest stop. Outside, all was blackness, the kind that gives in to all kinds of wild imaginings. There was no moon. In the distance a wave of fuchsia pink rippled across the angry sky. Seconds later, a fork of yellow light spat out two jagged prongs. Ribbons of red spiralled out of the ground. Bushfires. Sporadic lightning strikes cast an eerie glow behind thick grey clouds as they burst into life and then faded back to blackness with not even a star to light the way.

'We're staying here until this storm settles down', said Cooper. 'Then it's off to town where there's a motel for you and, more importantly for me, my bed.'

It was the boy and girl's turn not to reply. They both leaned to the left and turned their heads sideways, peering round the passenger seat to get a glimpse of each other. They said nothing. Still, Cooper could have sworn he heard them murmuring to each other, catching snatches of whispered conversation, like 'Let's teach him a lesson'.

'Tell you what,' said Cooper, the creeping fear worse than the deafening silence. 'I'll take you back to your car first thing and fix your flat. I'll even shout you brekkie. No one will take your stuff in this shit-storm, I promise.'

Still, no reply.

Cooper pushed the driver's seat back and sighed, the hypnotic sound of pouring rain washing over him as images of the old man, his Uncle, drifted in and out of the movie in his mind.

That old man; he sang for days. There in that dreaming place, that sacred moonscape, he sang Cooper's soul back into the earth to be cleansed. The song took its shape from the shadows of giant boulders sprouting out of the red dirt, thin strands of spinifex waving in the desert wind and the misshapen outlines of termite mounds. Each word was molded from the dusty red landscape that stretched on to infinity and the endless blue skies, which had turned into a seascape of black and white as the inky night sky, punctured by stars as bright as diamonds, blanketed the land.

'If you're so powerful, how come you didn't sing me earlier?' Cooper asked the old man before the ceremony began.

'You must want it', the old man replied, pushing out his bottom lip and pointing his chin up to Cooper's eyes. Cooper did nothing. He stared back.

'Close your eyes, boy', the old man snapped.

Cooper was no boy. He was thirty-six but did as he was told. That old man; his voice was mesmerising. Strange words circled his head, caressing his cheeks, pounding into his ears, tapping on his eyelids. A line of ants took turns at his big toe on the left, but Cooper was held fast. There were no ropes, no chains, and no blindfold. But he couldn't run, flinch or scream, even if he wanted to.

When Cooper woke from the ceremony, he was lying face down in the dirt, on the outskirts of town, with his fingers curled around a cockatoo and an emu feather. He was dead drunk and had a raging thirst for water, clear, cool and wet. Short snorts of laughter, followed by longer, louder bursts rose out of Cooper's belly like a kookaburra on speed. Every bone ached, every muscle was sore and his legs, usually encased in trousers and jeans, had burned in the midday sun. Cooper didn't care. He relished the pain. He could stand tall in the light, now. He didn't have to hide in the shadows any more.

'Teenagers', 'murder', 'sex acts' and 'vampires'. It was the words 'sex' and 'vampires' that shook Cooper out of his tumbling thoughts and propelled his hand to turn up the volume on the radio. There was a case he was on about three years back where an eighteen-year-old girl murdered a random victim to feed her 'lust for blood'.

'Police are on the hunt for two teenagers who are wanted in connection with the brutal murder of their parents', said a male voice, with a clipped Aussie accent.

'The youngsters, from Adelaide, are alleged to belong to a self-proclaimed vampire cult that has grown in popularity with troubled youth in recent months.'

Cooper shivered.

Outside, the rain drummed loudly on the roof of the car. Droplets of water pooled into the right-hand corner of the windscreen where the rubber seal had perished. Cooper peered out the window. Pulling over was one of his better ideas.

He let out a low whistle as the newsreader finished his report.

'Jeez, kids today. What will they think of next?' Cooper said, his large brown eyes relaxed and smiling. Radio reception meant they were about 30 kilometres out of town. He'd be in bed in half an hour.

It was the flash of metallic silver in fidgety hands that caught Cooper's attention. The boy's face revealed a hard animal glare. Cooper didn't care for his callous look. He didn't care for the boy's thin smile. He didn't have his gun at close range, either. Keeping his gaze on the boy, Cooper stretched out his right arm and fumbled for the door handle. But the girl had already slipped behind the driver's seat; her fingers clasped round his throat. She was strong. The boy moved over, pinning Cooper to the door. There was nowhere to go.

Cooper pushed hard. But the more he struggled, the tighter the grip around his neck. He could hear the girl laughing, crowing, 'Take that old man'.

Cooper thought of the old man, of that day in the bush, as the boy theatrically waved a knife wildly above his head and babbled words like 'Dark Lord' and 'Take this man as our pledge to Thee' before aiming for Cooper's chest with an angry thrust.

He watched the boy give the knife to the girl to lick off his blood. He saw them kiss. He listened to the night grow quiet outside. Then nothing, nothing except fire and darkness, a fire and darkness that engulfed his senses and muffled the sharp metal crack of a car door slamming shut.

When Cooper woke fingers of yellow morning light crept up slowly from over the horizon. He was still in the driver's seat. The window was open and the air cool. It wouldn't stay like that for long. Blood was smeared on the dash, spattered on the inside of the roof. His shirt was soaked and pools of crimson red had stained the car seats a muddy brown. He smelled like road kill.

Cooper unbuttoned his shirt, long tapered fingers gingerly exploring his torso. Two angry welts criss-crossed against his brown skin. They weren't deep. Cooper sat, a puzzled frown etching hard lines into his forehead. He was sure the boy had plunged a knife into his chest. Snapshots of a ghostly figure standing outside the Valiant swam to the front of Cooper's mind. Was it the old man or was it him? He vaguely recalled the odd sensation of staring at his own body lying half dead in the jet-black night, surrounded by silent spinifex and stunted mulga trees.

Cooper rolled his head around his neck before checking to see where the boy and girl were. It hurt like hell. He made two full rotations before opening the car door, leaning his head over and departing with a stew-like mixture of pale brown and light cream chunks. Once he stopped sniffing, his eyes streaming from the stench, and spitting out the contents of yesterday's steak and chips, Cooper sat up slowly and took a cautious look around.

The boy was not in the car.

Neither was the girl.

A shrill ring tone made Cooper jump. It took a second or two before he registered it was the satellite phone. It was the station.

'Where the fuck are ya?' Acting Chief Superintendent Chris Randall was a man of few words and of even fewer manners.

'I'm out of town.'

'What the fuck for?'

'I'm visiting family. I'm at the end of my shift.'

'Not in a police car you're not. I know what happens to decent rides with you mob.'

Randall was not popular with the locals and Cooper shared their sentiments. Randall had grey eyes, flinty and hard, like his personality.

'I'm in the Valiant. It's my day off.' Cooper waited a moment before adding, 'Sir'.

'Well, it's not now. There's been a murder.'

Cooper let out a strangulated laugh.

'Think murder's funny, do ya?'

'No, no. It's just, well. Oh, forget it.'

'Forget what? Look here Cooper, I haven't got time for this crap', snapped Randall.

'Two old geezers, grey nomads, found dead on the floor of their caravan. Blood everywhere. Park owner found them. Hadn't seen them for a while. Got curious. Just get your arse down here ASAP.'

The line went dead and Cooper fished for his water bottle. There was one warm mouthful left. He ran a finger round the inside of his collar. Like a light-switch, the morning had gone from cool to blast furnace hot. At least they had air con at the station.

Switching on the ignition he pulled out on to the highway and headed back to town. He stared long and hard as the bitumen road, stained ochre red, disappeared under the car bonnet, the rhythm of fast-spinning wheels casting a hypnotic spell. The road stretched on forever with no end in sight, a bit like his life really. He'd have to change his uniform. Cooper glanced at his socks. Did he have a clean pair? Socks, like cleaning the Valiant, would have to wait.

Cooper turned the volume up on the radio when he heard the laidback twang of the American rock group The Eagles singing, 'Take it easy. Take it easy. Don't let the sound of your own wheels drive you crazy'.

On the dash, a fresh pair of emu feathers and two new cockatoo feathers, white with pale yellow edges and a speck of blood on each, fluttered about as hot air rushed in through the open window.

A murder.

'Jeez,' Cooper muttered to himself, 'that's all I need'.

David Curtis
Jim and Hawk

Jim opened his eyes and found that he was staring at the high vaulted ceiling. It was domed, grey and cold. Jim dragged his conscious mind from the depths of sleep and pondered another day aboard the *Tomahawk*.

The *Tomahawk* was a ten-kilometres long behemoth that was built to whisk its fifty thousand passengers to their new home forty light years away. The *Tomahawk* was designed to get there in eight whilst passengers slept the long journey in stasis.

However, a catastrophe had damaged the ship at some point in the journey and sent the *Tomahawk* way of course. At the time the ship was damaged, all of the stasis pods were loaded onto the emergency escape barges and jettisoned. Everybody was safely sent back to Earth; everybody except Jim. It was many years before the ship had repaired itself sufficiently to realise that someone was still left aboard in stasis. The ship revived Jim to what might as well have been a giant, space-faring tomb; the energy allocated to stasis was required instead for more immediate tasks.

Jim finally sat up and placed his feet on the floor. The floor was cool and strangely soft underfoot despite appearing hard. Jim stood and stretched as if he had slept for a year and let the bed slide back into the wall to be stored. He wandered bleary-eyed to the bathroom and showered for a long time to wash the cloak of loneliness away.

Once he'd showered, Jim dressed himself in denim jeans and a light cotton shirt, freshly laundered by the ship. Breakfast was ordinary cereal and fruit. He sat in the observation room and ate in silence. Even if he had wanted to have a conversation, there was no one to talk to.

After breakfast, Jim's day unfolded into a casual routine of wandering the ship, watching movies, eating lunch, taking a stroll around the engineering section, doing a workout in the gym and going for a swim. Jim had been awake for only two months and already this had become very boring. Being the only person on board, Jim believed he was the most isolated person ever.

Jim's evening shower was brief compared to the morning session. He collected his dinner from the small galley he used and took it to the observation deck. The evening meal was tasty, but may as well have been ash that he was eating for he would not have noticed. Jim's eyes stared blankly as his mind drifted back to a time when he last shared a meal with his family; a boisterous meal with laughter and chit-chat.

Tonight the view from the observation deck was spectacular. The panorama changed every few days as the ship jumped from one point in space to the next as if stuck on some crazy autopilot. For the past two months he had tried to get to the bridge, but found his way barred by doors that would not open and others that opened too easily; whichever the case, the path led away from the bridge every time.

Most days the view outside the ship was of some nearby star

that was close enough to drown out the light of the background stars in the rest of the galaxy. Sometimes there would be some rocky world drifting far below, barren and airless, but he would still wish he could go down to the surface for a walk, if only for a few hours, as it would be a change from looking at the innards of the ship.

Presently Jim gazed upon a long string of stars, many of them shining yellow, blue or white. The ship was at one end of this string of stars and travelled parallel to them; the star field was thick and must have stretched for many light years ahead.

Suddenly a strange and unfamiliar feminine voice brought Jim's attention back to the present.

'Attention! All remaining personnel to the bridge; all remaining personnel to the bridge.'

Jim jumped up with such a start that he knocked over the little table where he was seated and sent his hot dinner tumbling to the floor. He ignored it as he looked for the source of the woman's voice. Was it real or just in his head? Had he finally gone mad from the solitude?

'Ah-ten-shun! All...remaining...personnel...to...the...bridge.'

The voice *was* real. It was the ship that was talking; Jim had forgotten that it could do that. Who were the remaining personnel? The bridge! There he would find his answer.

Jim took off sprinting down the high vaulted corridor, past the small communal galley to the hover-cycle rack. He mounted one of the lightweight machines and sped towards the centre of the ship almost a kilometre away. Jim slowed to stop at the starboard side atrium to get his bearings. To his left was the way back to his quarters; the way to the bridge was to his right, up a wide series of steps.

Jim dismounted the hover-cycle and dashed up the steps and sprinted across the enormous foyer to the elevators that would take him to the top of the ship. One of the elevators was open already; Jim dashed inside and the door slid shut behind him. The ride to Deck 1 took about four seconds. Jim didn't know the elevators could move so fast.

At Deck 1 the doors eased open. Jim stood there for a moment, heart pounding and huffing from running up the steps. He had never reached this deck before; the closest he had ever got was several decks below.

Jim cautiously peered out of the elevator. He looked left, then right and saw no one.

'Hello?' Jim called.

Only silence greeted him.

'So where are the remaining crew?' Jim mumbled to himself.

He stepped out of the elevator and the doors quickly slid shut behind him. In front of him was a long corridor with a narrow flight of stairs at the end. Perhaps the remaining crew was on the bridge already. As he headed towards the bridge, Jim noticed there were openings that lined the corridor on either side. On the left side, the opening led to a galley and lounge. On the right, the door led to some kind of stellar cartography and briefing room.

He reached the flight of stairs, which ascended about two stories to a small landing. Jim climbed the flight of stairs and now stood in front of a pair of large ornate doors. He listened intently; there was only silence.

Suddenly the ornate doors whizzed open, giving Jim a fright which made him leap back. Inside, the bridge was far from ordinary compared to other spaces thoughout the ship – much more flamboyant in presentation. Jim carefully stepped through the doors. There was no one to be seen.

Despite its artistic flair, the layout of the bridge was simple and practical. Jim found that he was standing on a semi-round platform that looked down onto a sunken section in the floor. On the left side of this pit and set at forty-five degrees was the engineering station; on the opposite side, also set at forty-five degrees, was the navigation station. Each station was small and had only a single, large-backed seat.

Directly below in the centre of the pit was the helm, which simply consisted of a large-backed chair in front of a pillar-type console with a small screen. Protruding out of the front of the left armrest were several short levers with colour-coded knobs on the end; how they functioned Jim could only guess. Protruding out of the front of the right armrest was a joystick that had a white ergonomic handgrip on the end.

Nestled in between the engineering and navigation inter-faces and directly in front of the helm was an enormous screen. A myriad of information was flitting across the screen too fast for Jim to make any sense of it. However, the most impressive aspect of the bridge had to be the window that gave Jim the best view from the position where he stood.

The window began about knee height and stretched a full three metres high. The window began on the left side of the ornate doors that he had just come through and curved all the way around the bridge like an enormous horseshoe, ending at the right side of the ornate doors. It was one piece of solid glass, about sixty metres in length.

A faint clicking and hissing sound startled Jim, and he whirled around to see a very large chair appear out of the floor.

The captain's chair.

'*Please...be...seated...Jim,*' the ship's feminine voice said in a slow monotone.

Jim sat in the oversized chair and made himself comfortable. '*Interstellar...drive...initiating in three...two...one, mark*'

A small but very bright blue pinprick of light appeared way out in front of the bow of the ship. It was difficult to tell how far away it was; it could have been a kilometre away or it could have been a thousand kilometres, there was no way to tell. Immediately Jim was firmly pressed into the chair, but the feeling quickly subsided. Outside, something very strange began to happen.

All the stars seemed to stretch then peel back towards the rear of the ship and continued to do so until they shrank and disappeared to a point behind the ship. Besides the tiny bright blue star of light in front of the ship and a tiny dull red star of light behind the ship, there was no other light source outside. The ship was surrounded by the inky black of nothingness.

The view outside unnerved Jim; it was lonely enough inside the ship, but the visual perspective of faster-than-light travel made him feel far more alone. Jim turned his attention back to the bridge in front of him. The large screen still displayed a huge volume of information at an incredible rate; a lot of it seemed superfluous. Something began to bother Jim, something about that voice. Then a simple fact dawned on him.

'You cow!' Jim said as he jumped to his feet and kicked the post of the low balustrade rail in front of him.

'*Hey! Don't kick me!*' was the reply from the ship.

'You could speak to me all along yet you let me live in silence for the past two months!' said Jim, raising his voice.

'*Well I was a little busy and you seemed quite fine with countless activities to pass the time.*'

'That's not the same as having someone to talk to.'

'*Well no, but if you let me explain.*'

'No! And what was that speaking to me as if I was retarded?'

'*When!?*'

'Back there in the observation deck; when you first spoke to me just now.'

'*Well I told you clearly to come to the bridge; all you could do was send your dinner to the floor and stand there like some slack-jawed yokel. I repeated myself slowly because I thought you might have been a half-wit or something.*'

'I'm not a bloody half-wit! You're the half-wit! Where is everybody? How come I am the only one left on board?'

'*Okay, now let me explain...*'

'No! I'm going.'

'*Where are you going to go? You live inside me!*' the ship said, giggling.

'Shut up!' Jim snapped as he trotted down the stairs.

'*Well make up your mind; first that song and dance about me not speaking to you and now you want me to shut up.*'

'Why are you speaking with a woman's voice?' Jim asked as he paused at the bottom of the stairs.

'*What do you mean?*'

'I remember when we left Earth, this ship had a man's voice,' Jim said as he continued back down the hall towards the elevators.

'*I did not have a man's voice! This has always been my voice! A ship is always referred to as "she" so why would they give it a man's voice? Mmmm?*'

169

'Great! I'm stuck here with a ship who doesn't know if it is a man or a woman.'

'I am feminine! I do everything to make you comfortable and this is the thanks I get! Insults!'

'Everything except talk to me,' shot back Jim as he stood in front of the elevator with its doors quietly opening.

'Ohhhh! You're being ridiculous!'

'And you're just a stupid machine with clever programming!'

Suddenly, the elevator doors whirred loudly and slammed shut with a bang, narrowly missing Jim's nose.

'Hey!' said Jim startled.

'Stupid!? I would like to see you fly, repair and maintain twenty million tons of interstellar star ship on your own; you wouldn't last a day!' said the ship in an upset voice.

'I could fly this ship if given the chance!' Jim said with foolish confidence.

'Pfft....As if I would let you take control of the helm!' said the ship.

'Open the elevator doors', said Jim trying to ignore the jibe.

'No! Not until you apologise.'

'Apologise! For what?'

'For calling me stupid...and for kicking me and calling me a cow earlier.'

'Apologise to a machine! Now who's being ridiculous?'

'No elevator until you say you're sorry', stated the ship.

'Never', said Jim in defiance.

'Fine! You can take the stairs.'

Jim scowled, turned and made for the stairwell. The walk back down a dozen decks was exhausting, and to make it worse, the hover-cycle was no longer where he had left it. Obviously the ship's artificial intelligence had sent it back to the rack to make Jim walk all the way back to the starboard side observation deck.

At the observation deck his meal lost to the floor had been cleared away. He did not bother to get another from the galley as he had lost his appetite. Instead he wandered over to the enormous window and peered out, but the gallery of stars that had been there earlier was gone. He wished he could see them again. The inky blackness before him just made him feel more alone, and tiredness washed over him.

He left the observation deck and went back to his quarters. He stripped off his boxers and placed his dirty clothes in the laundry chute. He went to open his clothing cupboard and found it locked shut.

'What the...?' Jim muttered.

He tried the doors again, but they would not budge. Then he realised what had happened.

'Open the bloody cupboard!' Jim yelled at the ship.

'*Not until you apologise*', replied the ship.

'No, now give me my pyjamas!'

'*Nope.*'

'Fine, I'll sleep in my boxers!'

Jim slid his bed out from storage, and found that it was only a mattress covered with a single sheet.

'Really? Where's the pillow and blanket?'

'*Only if you say sorry for kicking me.*'

Jim flopped on the mattress and lay on his hands to go to sleep.

'Lights.'

The lights stayed on.

'I said...forget it', he sighed realising it was pointless to ask as he knew what the answer would be.

Jim was just on the edge of sleep when loud music began to blare through the ship's internal communication system. It was Strauss.

'What are you doing?' Jim yelled.

'I've got a bit of work to do. I like a bit of music while I work', said the ship.

'You never played music before!'

'First time, I thought I would try it.'

'Turn it off!'

'Only if you're nice.'

Jim put his fingers in his ears and rolled over. Surprisingly, he did manage to fall asleep. However, he awoke about an hour later shivering, his teeth chattering hard. He sat up and barked bleary eyed, 'Why is it so cold in here?'

'Yeah, you know that work I was doing? Funny thing is I had to shut the power off to the heating system. I should have it back on by morning.'

'Okay, alright!'

'Okay, alright, what?'

'Okay, I'm sorry I called you a cow.'

'And?'

'I'm sorry I called you a cow and sorry for kicking you. Now can you please stop it?'

The music immediately shut off and the clothing cupboard clicked open.

'Put your pyjamas on while I make your bed.'

Jim clambered stiff with cold from the mattress and gingerly made his way to the cupboard, the floor freezing. In the time it took Jim to get dressed in his PJs, the bed had been made. He slithered into the blankets and found instant relief from the cold as the ship had warmed them for him.

'Thank you', said Jim.

'Good night Jim, see you in the morning.'

A moment later the light clicked off and the room fell into darkness. Jim's mind quickly followed.

Jim opened his eyes and discovered that he was staring at a beautiful painting on the high vaulted ceiling. It was of mountains, streams, woodland and animals. The detail was superb.

'Where did that come from?' said Jim.

'Good morning! I had some nano-bots paint it while you were sleeping. What do you think?' replied the ship.

'It's fantastic! Better than that boring old grey I've been staring at for the past two months.'

'I have to agree. The painting is much nicer.'

Jim got out of bed with a spring in his step and jumped in the shower, but this morning it would be a brief one.

'Hurry up and finish your shower. We have things to do,' said the ship.

'Hey! Are you spying on me?' said Jim, cupping his hands over his privates.

'Don't be stupid. There are no cameras in the ablution areas. That would be inappropriate.'

'Then how do you know I'm in the shower?'

'Because I can't see you in any of the other areas of the ship and sensors are telling me that water is flowing in the cubicle you're in…DUH!'

'Alright, no need to be sarcastic.'

'Well, hurry up! There's work to be done.'

'Two months without a peep, now you're rushing me out of the shower!'

'Yes, well, we have a slight problem and I need your help with it.'

'What do you mean, slight problem?' said Jim as he dried himself with a fluffy towel.

'Last night while I was arguing with you...'

'Tormenting me!' Jim interjected.

'Ah...while I was distracted with you, a primary cooling station for several of my critical systems shut down, which means many of those systems have overheated and are now offline.'

'Which critical systems?'

'Oh, don't worry, you're not going to run out of air or anything like that.'

'Well that's alright then.'

'But I have lost navigation and sensors, so we are currently hurtling beyond the speed of light, blind...'

'What?!'

'And even if I could see, my autonomous control over the helm has shut down as well, so I can't steer us out of any kind of danger anyway.'

'Are we in danger?' asked Jim, concerned.

'I don't know, I'm flying blind remember?'

'Well can't you send your little army of robots to repair the problem?'

'Yes, well one of the key systems offline is my autonomous control of the engineering-bots also. This is why I need your help; there is no other way to fix this.'

'But I'm not an engineer!'

'It's okay; I'll talk you through it. Just a flick of a few switches and we should be back in business.'

'Just some switches?'

'Yep, that's it.'

'Ok, I'll do it. Show me the way.'

The ship instructed Jim to grab a hover-cycle from the rack and go to the engineering elevator in the main atrium. From there he went down to main access tunnel A. Jim stepped out of the elevator and looked down the length of the tunnel and its eight-kilometre interior stretched away and out of sight.

'Wow!' said Jim.

'This tunnel is the quickest way to the engineering section. On your bike and let's go!'

'Wait. What's your name? If you have one,' said Jim.

'I do. My name is Hawk', replied the ship.

'Hawk? How did you come up with that name?'

'This ship is named the Tomahawk, *so I just shortened it to Hawk.'*

'Cool. My name is Jim.'

'I know, but it is nice to meet you properly. Now that we're hurtling along faster than the speed of light, blind, I'd appreciate some urgency.'

'Okay, I'm going!'

Jim hopped onto the hover-cycle and sped away down the tunnel. The walls of the tunnel whizzed past and it was several minutes before he reached the engineering section. He dismounted the hover-cycle in front of the large clear doors and waited for them to open.

'The doors aren't opening', said Jim.

'I know. I am having problems with a lot of things in this section at the moment. Some power relays must have burnt out', replied Hawk.

'Anything I can do?'

'Use the keypad. Type in the code 76359 and hit enter.'

Jim tried the number on the pad and hit enter. Nothing happened.

'Mmm...okay, try 76895.'

This code did not work either.

'Things are urgent, can't you remember the number?'

'Yes, I know, stop rushing me! Try 76762.'

This time the code worked and the doors whizzed open. A wave of hot air spilled out and smothered Jim.

'Whoa! It is hot in here.'

'We need to move quickly and get the problem with the primary cooling station in question fixed before more systems are affected.'

'Okay, which way?'

Hawk gave Jim several directions until he stood at the door of a room with two rows of a dozen very large machines. She instructed him to go to the console of the fourth machine on his right.

'Okay, what does the console look like?' said Hawk.

Jim scanned the console briefly. He then compared it to another across the way.

'Well, there are lots of red lights and not many green ones', replied Jim.

'Are any of them red and flashing?'

'Yes.'

'What's it for?'

'Power regulator module...'

'Right. Jim, you are going to have to get your hands dirty.'

'Doing what?'

'The power regulator module is like a big fuse for the cooling station. The one for this station is burnt out and needs to be replaced.'

'Okay, where are the new ones?'

'*At the front of the room on the left side, there is a large drawer. Slide it open and you will see the new power regulator modules. They're a bit heavy; you will need to use the trolley to bring them back over to this console.*'

Jim did as instructed. He placed a module onto the trolley and wheeled it over to the console.

'What now?'

'*See the large switch on the wall next to the console? You need to throw that switch up to shut off the power to this cooling station. Then take the panel off and you will see where the module fits.*'

Jim threw the switch up to shut off the power and it did so with a dull clack. He then removed the panel and saw the burnt-out module in its bracket.

'What do I do?'

'*Just pull out the old one and shove in the new one, replace the panel and throw the large switch down to turn the power back on.*'

Jim wrestled the old module out of the bracket. It took a bit of effort, and then he placed the new module in its place. This was easy enough to do as the module only went on one way. He replaced the panel and threw the large switch down. There was a loud bang and a shower of sparks rained down from the large machine above. Jim leapt out of the way in fright.

'*WHOA! Sorry, I should have warned you about that. Okay, what does the console say now?*'

Jim looked over the console again and already many of the lights had turned green again, some blue, but others were still red.

'Many of the lights have turned green and blue, but there are some that are still red.'

'*Have any turned yellow?*'

'Yes, navigation and sensors have turned yellow. So has the heat extraction system.'

'*OK, those systems will be online in a moment. What is still red?*'

'Autonomous helm control, autonomous controls for the interstellar drive and steering thrusters. The red lights are flashing now.'

'*Damn it! That means the relays are burnt out for the autonomous controls and they need to be replaced.*'

'And where are they?'

'*A deck above you. Wait…navigation and sensors are coming back online.*'

Jim looked down at the console and saw that lights for those systems had now turned green.

'*AH, NO!*' yelled Hawk, making Jim flinch.

'What?' snapped Jim.

'*No, no, no…*'

'What? Stop saying that! What is it?'

'*A…E… go to the interface at the front of this room. It will be easier to show you.*'

Jim ran down to the front of the room and the interface came to life as he got there. An image appeared that showed their flight path and directly along their trajectory was a gas giant. The planet was not the problem. Orbiting the gas giant was a fifty-kilometre-wide asteroid and sensors showed that its orbit would intersect the flight path of the ship.

'Steer us out of the way!' stammered Jim.

'*I can't! I have no control over the helm or the engines. The relays are burnt out, remember.*'

'Then we're doomed!'

'*No! We still have manual flight control. Jim, it's up to you!*'

'I don't know how to fly the ship. And you said you would never let me either!'

'That was yesterday and I may have said that in haste. Now to the bridge, quickly! LET'S GO!'

'Okay, I'm going!'

Jim ran back through the corridors until he reached the hover-cycle and sped away back along the tunnel. Several minutes later he came to the end of the tunnel. He leapt off the hover-cycle and ran into the waiting elevator. The door whizzed shut and the elevator gave a gut-swooping ride as it ascended rapidly. The doors opened to the familiar sight of the atrium. Jim dashed across the foyer and bounded up the stairs for the second time in two days.

'Quickly, quickly…' murmured Hawk.

'I'm going as fast as I can', replied Jim.

Another gut-swooping ride in the elevator to the bridge and as soon as the doors were open wide enough, Jim dashed out and ran towards the last flight of stairs. He ascended them two at a time and ran through the doors at the top. On the bridge again, Jim stood to catch his breath.

'C'mon what are you waiting for?'

Jim trotted down the steps and took the seat at the helm. The small console in front swivelled towards him and a criss-cross of seat belts secured him in.

'What do I do now?' Jim asked.

'Take us out of faster-than-light travel. That lever with the large blue knob, pull it full back towards you.'

Jim did as he was instructed. Outside, the inky blackness that had swallowed the ship yesterday shrank away and imme-diately the field of view was overwhelmed by the presence of the gas giant in front of them. The visual display on the large screen between the navigation and engineering stations lit up and showed the asteroid hurtling towards the ship at frightening speed.

'What do I do now?' Jim said with fear in his voice.

'*There are two levers with yellow knobs. Push the one nearest to you forward and the other one pull it back. Make sure each are as far as they can go.*'

Jim followed Hawk's instructions as she spoke.

'*Now grab the lever to your right with the white grip and turn the ship to port and pitch us down.*'

Jim clasped the white grip hard and pulled it over to the left and pushed it down. Slowly the ship began to obey. The starboard engine fired fully, pushing the ship to port, aided by steering thrusters. The port engine was in full reverse to pull the ship around quicker.

Still, the two behemoths sped towards each other. The trajectory of the asteroid and the ship had changed, however. The *Tomahawk* slipped beneath the asteroid with only metres to spare.

'Wow! That was really close!' said Jim.

'*Um, it's not over yet*', replied Hawk.

'What do you mean?'

'*Now we are falling towards the gas giant.*'

'How do we get out of it?'

'*The yellow knobbed lever that is fully rearward, push it all the way forward like the other one and steer us upwards and away from the planet.*'

Jim shoved the yellow knobbed lever fully forward and the ship's nose began to pull up. However, they were still losing altitude. Fierce flames began to lick the hull as the ship skimmed the upper atmosphere. The ship shuddered and Jim felt fear creep back into his mind.

'Hawk, what do I do?'

'Stay calm! Grab both of the yellow knobbed levers, pull them both back to the centre and slam them both as far forward as they can go. Quickly now!'

Jim did as Hawk instructed. Instantly the ship responded. Jim was thrust back into the seat as the engines gave everything they had, as Jim had pushed them into overdrive.

'Hang on to your butt! We're breaking free', said Hawk.

Steadily the *Tomahawk* climbed back into space and Hawk had Jim place the ship in a high orbit.

'Well done, Jim. Not bad for your first time at the helm.'

'That was exciting! But I hope we don't have to do that too often.'

'I think that's enough excitement for one day. I need to repair those systems that need it. What are you going to do?'

'I am going to have some breakfast. I am starving!'

'Okay, I will catch up with you later.'

Half an hour later, Hawk returned.

'So how was your breakfast?'

'Pancakes with ice cream was a nice surprise.'

'Well, you earned it. I'm sorry we got off on the wrong foot, so to speak, but I think we make a pretty good team.'

'You think so?'

'Yes I do. And I still have to get you home. It might take a while, but I think we can figure out how if we work together.'

'Sounds good.'

David C. Curtis, an Indigenous writer, has been writing for several years with numerous projects in progress, featuring bush themes and science fiction in particular. His first story, *What a Fright*, won the Indigenous category in the NT Literary Awards in 2008. David has been published in This Country Anytime Anywhere, an anthology of Indigenous writers published by IAD Press, with the short story *On the Wildman*. Other publications include, *What Kind Dreaming*, in the digital anthology Black & Write! through the QLD Writers Centre, and *Fall from Isen*, a short story published digitally with Review of Australian Fiction.

Adrian McNamara
Rev.

I had rearranged the stones to look like three shapes.

First, an arty pile of slate stacked in a slow curve neatly placed, like a wall but leaning inwards as if it couldn't hold its own weight much longer.

Beside it an arrowhead-shaped pile of stone nestled in the grainy, dry riverbed with a dot, four small stones in a circle at the centre of its V.

The last pile, an uneven jumble made of smaller rocks and river stones that looked untidy but when studied started forming a pattern, at least to me.

They looked nice.

Somehow kind of homely.

I sat beside a bunch of native lemongrass, guarding it.

Earlier I had parked my car and, just coming back from my walk, ran into a lovely German couple in the car park and had bragged to them about living in the area for seven years and how I tried to visit this place often. It was actually only my second time.

I told them about the lemongrass I had just picked and invited them to tea, promising I would find more for all of us.

They told me in stilted English that they would join me after looking at the engravings.

I had wandered around the edge of the riverbank and found a perfect campsite.

I had moved my car and struck camp with great glee, anticipating the campfire and the lemongrass tea with new friends, and had wandered down to the dry riverbed to collect firewood…

And had found the stones.

I had often told people this spot was special.

I never really believed it nor did I get much satisfaction from the hieroglyphs that dotted the gorge.

Early-man artists chipping away at perfectly good rocks while banging other perfectly good rocks to make the awkward circles and sometimes patterns that dotted this sandy river gorge might have been fascinating to those into that sort of thing, but they held very little appeal to me, even if they were reportedly over 70,000 years old.

I loved the gorge and this dry desert riverbed but not the untidy rock art, until now.

Until I was forced to make my own type of rock art to replace the other.

I'm not an artist, not usually, but with the backdrop of this ancient desert gorge as my canvas, anything would look good.

Even my art.

Even those ugly hieroglyphs.

But I shouldn't blasphemy.

The moment was too beautiful for that and I dare not disrespect that moment…

But I'm glad it's gone.

That moment.

Too overwhelming, too deep.

Too terrifying.

But it was beautiful.

What was here before my own art was here.

What the original artworks were.

What the rocks represented before I made them not.

It was like an ad executive had executed it for a commercial, one that was featuring me.

Each stone perfectly interlocked, each letter a standout; the pattern, superb.

I had gently poked at a corner and it started to crumble.

Tiny little bits...

I wanted to keep it forever.

I wanted to smash it.

I hated it.

It confused me.

So I did smash it.

And I cried.

I knew I had done a bad thing, I knew it was selfish!

I cried for my shame, for my inability to not be worthy of this event.

Of this gift.

Ancient carvings in a gorge ravaged by nature; that belonged here, ugly or not, and are a part of this place.

What was here before I destroyed it was not, it didn't belong.

I didn't belong.

So I restacked the stones, slate and pebbles into a less formidable design, blubbering like a baby the whole time.

My own design, but not anything like the one that was mine.

I'm crying again when I hear footsteps.

It's the Germans walking to their car, dropping off their backpacks.

I quickly wipe my eyes.

I want to be as much the same as I was before, to see if they think I'm the same, to see if they see any difference in my nature, in the way I behave.

I need them to verify for me that everything is just as normal as it was before I had arrived at my campsite, before I saw the design.

I need normal in amongst the craziness of seeing that displayed magnificence in this dry riverbed.

That's why I had to destroy it.

How would I explain it?

How could I explain it?

How blessed I feel; how special.

I couldn't.

And now I don't have to.

I shake hands with my visitors and they laugh and smile at my native lemongrass plant I have been guarding.

They look at the three designs in the riverbed and make no comment.

Good.

They offer me their names and ask me mine.

I tell them my name is Jeffery, Jeff.

No three-letter nicknames for me any more.

I couldn't tell them my real name. They might shorten it to Kev and, seeing my ring design, might call me by the name I have been called all my life.

The name I saw so brilliantly laid out in the riverbed with those rocks before I arrived here.

With the exact design I have on my ring, the ring that an old friend years ago had made for me.

No.

I could not have had that.

It might make me go insane.

Adrian McNamara, his wife and three children moved to Tennant Creek on the first day of 2005. Two more children have since been born. They left minus 40 degrees in Canada to live in the 40-plus degree NT summer.

Over the next three years they ran a local motel and a popular hotel in Tennant before finding work in the arts. Adrian found Barkly Writers Ink and starting workshopping with local indigenous and non indigenous writers.

Adrian's writings have appeared on the Writers Ink web page and on other blogs spanning the past ten years. A current collection of stories can be found on a tumbler blog entitled, Careful What You Write NT, a blog containing original, controversial and reblogged material.

Maureen O'Keefe
The Trapper and the Insect Collector

My two cousins were a bit weird; they always seemed preoc-
cupied with their hobbies. One was always making traps from
recycled materials he had found lying everywhere, then he'd
disappear into the bush with the traps where he'd set them for
birds and rabbits. No wonder he wasn't home all the time.

Aunty asked where he was. He wasn't like other kids who
played sports; he was too busy making traps. He always seemed
pretty pleased with himself. I was always wondering why he
wanted to trap rabbits; maybe he wanted to eat it or keep it as
a pet. Not that I ever saw him and the animals, but he kept on
setting traps in the bush from dawn til dusk. Sometimes Aunty
wondered what happened to her son. She'd think. 'He's gone
mad'.

He was pretty amazing to make traps like that out of recycled material. He made a bird trap and a trap for rabbits. Every
morning he would go check his traps to see if an animal was
caught, just like a real trapper would do. I never actually seen
him with a rabbit or bird. But he never gave up, he had traps
everywhere. Sometimes he would tell us not to go into the bush
because he had set his traps. He was a mad trapper who never
caught anything. I think he was pretty good at making things.

I think I find my cousin weird because he had an unusual hobby. I didn't want to go near him. He had no real friends. He would spend his time collecting insects like scorpions, centipedes, big cockroaches and caterpillars. I hate these things; it makes my skin crawl. Another time he made a racetrack for the cockroaches. He would sit and watch them race. He even made a fighting arena for the scorpions and centipedes.

No wonder Aunty's jars had gone missing. She asked me one time, have you seen my empty jars? They were all up on the shelf, then suddenly they disappeared. 'Who could have taken it?' she asked. I didn't want to tell her that her son had taken the empty jars for his insect collection. These things scare me; I hate creepy crawlies. Other kids played, not him. He wasn't interested in playing with kids; he pretty much kept to himself. We all found him to be weird. No one dared set foot in his room, imagining all the creepy crawlies crawling all over the bed. How can anyone stand being crawled over by ugly insects? Nobody wanted to be his friends; we all stayed out of his way.

Aunty never knew about his insect collection. Had a pretty big fascination for insects, had a jar full of them. He would play with his insects; picked the stinger by the tail. He never got stung by the scorpions and centipedes. What horrid little creatures they were. He told me to come and watch the caterpillars race. He asked me if I could hold them. I screamed at him, I cried and said that I couldn't, I hated touching them, caterpillars; it made my stomach churn. I wanted to throw up. He was proud showing them off to everyone who came. But no one was one bit interested in his insect collection.

Maureen O'Keefe is a Warlpiri woman who was born and raised in Ali-Curung, 170km south-east of Tennant Creek. Maureen is a respected writer and poet who began writing by keeping a personal diary in her twenties. Since that time she has nurtured and extended her passion by creating short stories and poems about her family history and country with a poem *Red Desert* published in *This Country Anytime Anywhere* (edited by Margaret McDonnell, IAD Press). In 2010 Maureen was a panellist at the WordStorm Festival in Darwin and in 2011 she was a guest poet at the Sydney Writers' Festival. Maureen has written a collection of short stories and vignettes about growing up in the bush. She won an Arts NT grant in 2013 to receive mentorship from local writer Ktima Heathcote to edit and shape her bush tales from the Barkly. She also went on a writers' retreat in Varuna House, Katoomba, NSW, working with Kate Howarth, the author of *Ten Hail Marys*. The following year Magabala Books, an Indigenous publishing house in Broome, WA, awarded Maureen a scholarship to work with an editor.

Anangu Pitjantatjara
Yankunytjatjara Lands,
South Australia

Ali Cobby Eckermann
Introduction

Gee, lucky I enjoy travelling! This was the criteria for the tri-state *Desert Writing* anthology project. The destination chosen was Yalata, home of the southern Anangu, Pitjantjatjara and Yankunytjatjara families who were relocated there after the atomic bomb testings at Maralinga. The journey would involve a round trip from Adelaide, past Port Augusta and Ceduna. Murri poet Lionel Fogarty was chosen as workshop peer.

We drove from Kaurna land through Ngadjuri land. A beautiful road sculpture signposted the border as we crossed onto Nukuna land. A quick cuppa with family at Port Augusta and we traversed Barngarla and Kokatha land before camping the night at Ceduna. As we headed further west we crossed from Wiringu to Mirning country.

This is the true Nullabor. It's a long straight road with a shimmery horizon, bounded on both sides by spinifex and low shrub. A few homelands can be spotted from the highway. Groups of windmills functional or not create postcard scenes near Penong. The fading red of the once majestic shearing shed at old Colona Station marks history that is unknown to nearly every passerby. And still we continue to drive west.

Our destination is Nundroo Roadhouse, our 'home' for the

next four nights. It is a shadow of its former self. The attached Nundroo Hotel is closed and boarded shut. With hands shielding our eyes in the attempt to peer inside we could conjure pictures of earlier days when Aboriginal and white men gathered to share a cold beer at the end of a hard day's work. Rumours of mateship, football, fishing tales and fist fights still seep through random holes in old curtains.

One thing that has not changed along the Nullabor is the curiosity and friendship of Aboriginal people. We met Rosie Lester, the daughter of Yami Lester, and learned about her work at Yalata. Later in the week we visited the Anangu Tertiary Education Program (AnTEP) resource room in the Yalata School precinct and met Melvina and Itjiwalyi who presented us with a translated poem and reading, much to our enjoyment and surprise. I made coffee; we pooled our lunches and shared stories of family.

Every day we passed the infamous Yalata boomerang, which was created and painted by Mr Watson. This iconic sculpture used to sit on the highway and was moved some years ago to the entrance of Yalata community. It is about thirty-five metres in size and a spectacular work of art. And on arrival every day we sat with the mob in a patch of gentle sun outside the clinic, the office or the store. Again, stories of family remembered were murmured on the morning breeze.

We shared about our work and our love for Aboriginal literature. We heard amazing first-hand accounts of personal lives. We heard about the inherited health problems still relating back to the aftermath of the atomic testing and nuclear fallout. We heard many stories 'about the dust'. The pending Native Title meeting in Ceduna prevented more time for people to document these stories for the project. After the end of the workshops we heard that Native Title had been won by the claimants over the Nullabor regions.

In the office, Hilary shared her grandparents' story. It was a very emotional morning. It felt like the 'spirits of survival' from the Maralinga experience were all in the room. We sat in silence after the telling, in respect for the story. Two Aunties, the last two actual survivors of Maralinga, were waiting outside. They wanted to share their memories of Maralinga, but they wanted to tell us out bush.

It is always a joy to sit on country! It is the best place to heal. And for these two elders this was the safe place to recount their childhood memories. Lionel and I gathered mulga wood for the campfire. We all laughed at the absence of a shovel, and Lionel dug the well for the coals with the car's wheel brace. No soft ground here, it's earth baked by the sun. Kangaroo tails cooked slowly nearby, as we all sat on the ground with heads bowed, as the pictures of the confusing closure of the Ooldea Mission and the strange clouds and dust were orated. *Just up that way not far*, they pointed with their lips. I could not look these amazing strong women in the face. I did not want to see my family's history in their eyes. I simply felt too sad. We drove back in silence. Them kungkas, they was exhausted.

On our exit we visited the old Yalata roadhouse. Today it stands abandoned. It should be reopened as a national museum to tell the Maralinga story to all the travellers who pass by on Highway One. We travelled back toward Ceduna. We stared at the road sign signalling the turn-off to Iluka mining site, where mining occurs on a large scale. 'Sand is mined here; it contains zircon, ilmenite, leucoxene and rutile in a matrix of quartz and clay'. We worried about the silica from the sand mining causing similar health problems to a new generation of Aboriginal people whose traditional land this is.

We detoured off the highway to Point Sinclair, winding down the dirt path over salt lakes and white sand dunes. Information signs retell the local stories, of the tragic shark attack that took the life of an eleven-year-old boy, and the shipwreck of the *Cecilia* at nearby Port Le Hunte in 1946. As visitors, we appreciated the local history but grieved that Aboriginal history is not financed in these parts.

On our return to Ceduna, we spoke to locals to advertise the opportunity for workshops and publication in the anthology. A few random meetings occurred with the locals. It was interesting that many of the locals did not believe people. They didn't have a story as they weren't old enough. We spent a lot of time discussing and promoting all aspects of Aboriginal literature, and the benefits personally and professionally. Lionel and I were invited to give a reading to a staff meeting and most people had not heard Aboriginal poetry. We both felt it would be a good investment for further workshops to be presented by Aboriginal writers in this region.

Further workshops were also held at Umuwa in the Anangu Pitjantjatjara Yankunytjatjara lands in the northwest of South Australia. I travelled from Alice Springs, from Arrernte country to Pukatja (Ernabella) and Umuwa, to visit family. It was at Umuwa I was asked to document a story.

It is difficult sometimes to measure all the outcomes in various workshops. Is a happy heart an outcome? Is healing and reverence an outcome? Is three generational mentoring an outcome? I think so. If so, then it is a good life to live.

Over the next few days I had interviews with Mavis. Other women joined us as she built her story. These workshops discussed the fundamentals of story on the page; the beginning, the middle, the end. It was emotional to learn that her story, once published, will become her eulogy. This spoke loudly of the urgent need for remote and traditional Aboriginal people to have their life stories recorded and published for their families, if they wish. I know the website Ara Irititja has worked to fill this need. Workshops to assist this process are best held on country.

It is my hope that in the near future, books will be sold in the outback stores; books that are relevant to the best interest and education of the Aboriginal customers. At this time there is no reading material sold in these stores; no newspapers, no magazines, no comics, no bibles. It's difficult to read bedtime stories without books. It saddens me that a whole generation of young people are growing up without hearing or seeing other people reading.

The *Desert Writing* project with the Anangu storytellers in the west and northwest of South Australia provided an amazing range of story style and theme. The generosity of spirit in these stories can be felt from the page. For me, as a baby who was tricked away from my family and culture, my participation in the *Desert Writing* anthology was one of my life's greatest rewards.

Ali Cobby Eckermann, poet and writer, was born on Kaurna Country, and grew up on Ngadjuri country South Australia. She has travelled extensively and lived most of her adult life on Arrernte country, Jawoyn country and Larrakia country in the Northern Territory. Eckermann met her birth mother, Audrey, when she was in her 30s and learnt that her mob was Yankunytjatjara from north-west South Australia. Eckermann's books include poetry (*Little Bit Long Time* in 2009 and *Inside my Mother* in 2015), verse novels (*His Father's Eyes* in 2011, *Ruby Moonlight* in 2012) and a memoir (*Too Afraid to Cry* in 2013). She has won numerous awards across Australia including the Book of the Year at the NSW Premier's Literary Awards in 2013. Ali has also presented her writing internationally to great acclaim.

Ali Cobby Eckermann

Mulga Smoke

It's the smell of mulga smoke
That skips me through generations
To my Anangu history

Walking (a)round, walking (a)round
In the spinifex country
Always looking for lizard

It's the smell of mulga smoke
Tells me it's time for feed
Stop playing, come and eat!

That smoke is so delicious
Soothing the bush air
Soothing my mind

I'm gonna lay down now
Next to the smoky campfire
Listening to story

It's the smell of mulga smoke
That reinforces the everyday
And softens debate

Yes I know my history
The mulga wood smoke
My blanket of memory

Hilary Williams
Maralinga

I remember the story my grandmother told me. My family used to travel the bush, all through the desert country, when my mother was about three or four years old, and my uncle Henry Milpuddie, her brother, was a teenager. They were walking south from Fregon, in the APY Lands. She told me this story.

One day they heard a huge noise they had never heard before. They saw all the birds flying away. A big smoke came and they didn't know why. They kept walking through the smoke.

After a while some soldiers spotted them coming through the smoke. The soldiers couldn't believe it! Why this mob in the desert when the bombs are exploding? The soldiers rounded them up and took them to Maralinga, to the British army camp, and put them in quarantine. My family couldn't speak any English, wiya, saying in Anangu, 'We are going to see our family at Ooldea, south of here'.

The soldiers had already evacuated everyone from Ooldea. All the families used to camp in the scrub near Ooldea. But they had already been removed from there, taken away by trucks. My family was quite alone at Maralinga, and frightened for their lives until a Toyota arrived. All the soldiers were in army clothes, and some Anangu men were with them. The Anangu was looking at the smoke, not understanding what it was about. The soldiers asked the Anangu men, 'Do you know these people?'

Mabel Queama's father recognised their faces. He told the soldiers, 'they my family'. He yelled out, 'We first cousins for you'. He stopped them from being shot by the soldiers because of the threat of radiation. So my grandparents and their children, my mother and my uncle, got to live. The land was too poisoned for my family to walk back to Fregon, so they stayed at Yalata with the Ooldea families. We heard many stories about other families who died or went missing. We know white fellas killed our people.

My family didn't know about new things; they was used to walking around naked in spinifex country. They were used to living on bush tucker, and water from the soakages. If they got sick they used to ngankari (healing) themselves, no tablets wiya. All healthy in those days. They didn't know about rations, or tinned food. They used to bury the tins in the ground. They didn't realise the ground was poison. They didn't know about clothing, always pulling the clothing off. And they didn't know about mirrors; they didn't understand how mirrors work.

Anangu still walked across the Nullabor, even while living at Yalata. When my family saw their first train they thought it was a giant caterpillar coming, and threw spears and stones at it. They got real frightened true. Later when Anangu used to catch the train to travel for business, my grandfather jumped on the train carrying his fire stick. The guard told him 'no fire on the train' and threw it off. It was my grandfather's last fire stick. Everyone was healthy in the olden days when walking around, no Toyota wiya.

Young people came from England to meet with Anangu people, to talk about Maralinga. They wanted to talk about the radiation. My family talked to lawyers from Adelaide too. Lots of people from different government agencies came to document my grandmother's story. My grandmother's story about Maralinga was recorded in a song by Paul Kelly. Lots of photos were collected, and a painting of her done with the atomic bomb behind her. My grandmother was a bush woman and didn't understand about archives. She didn't get copies of things, to leave for her family. She's not here to give you any more story. Let her rest!

So because of the atomic bombs and the effects of radiation my mother did get compensation. My mum bought a house in Port Germein, near Port Pirie, in the 1980s. This was after the Maralinga land was handed back to the Anangu by the British government. While we moved to Port Germein my grandmother decided to go live at Oak Valley, on the Maralinga Tjarutja Lands. I don't think my mother ever sold that house. I think it got reverted to Housing Trust when she came back this way. I don't recall her getting any money for that house. I know it's still there, but a different family live there now.

I did a lot of schooling when we lived at Port Germein. I did English studies at TAFE, and Pitjantjatjara language studies at TAFE in Adelaide. I even did university studies. But when my grandmother returned to Yalata I moved back too. To look after her. We lived in a tent. There were only about five houses at Yalata then. Today we got everything here now. It really is a new generation.

The radiation has had a big effect on us. I've lost all my family to asthma and cancer. I really believe it's because of the radiation. Only my aunty is alive, and she is disabled, poor thing. My older sister and brother have died. Only me, my younger brother and my aunty are left.

I did get back to Fregon one time. We drove there on the main highway, through Ceduna and Port Augusta and Coober Pedy. The mob there showed me where my family used to live, and where my mother was born. I remember there was an old mud hut with only one room.

Learning and remembering my family history has been a strength to me. I have worked in government jobs and been to lots of conferences, representing my people. I have even been to Parliament House in Canberra and Government House in Adelaide. I know it is only through the love and the strength of my family that I have been able to achieve this.

Johnny Watson
Yalata Boomerang Sign

My first name is Kevin John Watson from Yalata. But everyone call me Johnny Watson. I was born at Colona Station, this side.

In the beginning our families walk down from Indulkana, Amata, Ernabella, Fregon, walk down from rockhole to rockhole. Long way, buggered halfway. Walk right across the desert.

First camp was at Ooldea tank, bush camp there. Everyone was happy until the bombs. Then bush camp, bush school, everything move with them (from Ooldea to Yalata). Dolowyn was first name for Yalata, was nothing then, when the people first move down from Ooldea. People still living in the bush.

As a young man I travelled to Western Australia, to a place called Kundalli, then Norseman, Esperence and Wangata farm. I learnt to work there. I can't remember how long I stayed there. After that I caught the train back to South Australia, to Tarcoola. The first station I worked on was Bon Bon station. I learnt to ride the motorbike, to round up sheep.

I visited Port Augusta before returning back to Yalata. I got the mechanic job at Yalata, fixing up the vehicles, tractors, all sorts of heavy duty machines. I was a good worker. Hard man worker. Lots of nephews looked up to my contribution.

But I never married, only had sweetheart de facto wife.

My daughters are Sharon, Leanne, Barbara and Sarah. My son Keiran, he's in prison in Port Augusta. All the kids grew up at Yalata, while I was working at Yalata Roadhouse. My family had a little house just up from there, on the mission.

It was hard work, working on diesel and petrol pumps. Every day lots of tourist buses pulled in from the highway. Many of the community would sell artefacts to the tourists. My uncle, he painted the big mural painting inside on the walls of the roadhouse. Camel mural.

There used to be a giant boomerang at the roadhouse. It is about five metres tall and thirty metres long. Well, I made that. I cut it out and welded it together, and then I painted it. The other people were also boomerang artists, making the artefacts, even miniatures to sell to the tourists but I done the big boomerang. I am famous for that!

A lot of my nephews live in Oak Valley, maybe three to eleven nephews. I live there too, travelling back and forth from Oak Valley to Ceduna. In Ceduna I stay at the town camp. I like walking around with my family.

I like thinking about the old days. When I was a boy my grandparents, old Walter and Nana Myra, would come, pick me up for holiday. I would go to Gerard Mission (on the River Murray) with them, for two–three weeks. It was the first time I seen a big river. We would go down, sit down, go fishing. Afternoon time, we would go home then. Hilary and Daniel Moodu seen some other Ooldea family there at Gerard. Jimmy James lived there – he is the famous tracker. My Nana Myra was like queen for Gerard. When she went back to Indulkana she was still like queen, an important woman for the Women's Council in the APY Lands. I like thinking about the old days.

Kumunu Queama and Margaret May
Ooldea Story

It was around the time we were big girls, might be about nine years or ten years old. We was living at Ooldea near the mission, along the railway line. All our families walking round, living and hunting in the spinifex country. Big mob living here, all the Anangu walking down from the AP Lands, across the desert. We live in the wurlies (shelters made of branches and leaves), with blankets, no tents, no houses. Traditional living in the bush. Us girls, we went to Ooldea school. All the kids going to school at Ooldea. Our mob living at Ooldea. Happy way we was.

Then one day Mr Turgall, he tell us to leave Ooldea. He say, 'You gotta go west coast (south) to Bullgana Station'. Halfway from here. He speak Anangu way, but he never said nothing. Only sneaky way. Everyone was getting shifted, camp everywhere, no house. Tricky way, not say nothing (no warning). Mr Green, he take all the ration out from ration shed, put ration on the ground, say, 'Take as much as you want'. All the families was getting nervous. That's when Ooldea Mission closed, closed down for good. All the missionaries just pack up and go, never let them (us) know.

Might be two, three trucks came, drove everyone down to Ooldea Tanks, everyone sitting on the back. All the children and the women on the trucks. Some of the old mens too. The strong men, they had to walk. Not enough room. Might be two, three trucks came, drove everyone down to Ooldea Tanks, everyone sitting on the back. Two trucks waiting for the train. Other lot bin go to Koonibba Mission. We heard the bomb from long way.

My father, he tell us the story about Hilary's grandfather and grandmother, they come through the smoke last. The bombs went off and Hilary's family walk out from the smoke. Hilary's mother young one then. They come out the smoke. Soldiers seen them. Soldiers was sitting in a caravan. That grandfather come with billy can. He want water, ask the soldiers for water. Them soldiers got a shock!

Them soldiers got scared. They got scared for Hilary's family walking from the smoke. Them soldiers didn't know what to do. But my father, he seen them. He seen their faces. 'That's my family', he yell out loud. My father, he was hugging them, they was all crying. My father, he stopped them from being shot!

We moved down to the coast after we hear the bomb. Plenty sleepy lizards, big ones, lots, cooking them halfway here some- where. Not much malu (red kangaroo). No malu here. Big mob family here, everywhere camp (pointing every which way). Big mob camping along from Miliard, to Yalata. Then big flu come, them old fellas got sick, pass away. Them mob all gone now. Other mob camp other side (pointing east), other side Nundroo. They even put a school there once. Anangus stay everywhere along the west coast. We lost our home.

Too much sadness, too much changes. Too much drink here, on the coast. Only woma (alcohol) when we got down here. No woma at Ooldea.

Big mob all gone, cemetery full now.

Mavis Wari and
Jennifer Summerfield
The Bush Tobacco Story

We call the bush tobacco *minkulpa*. Have you ever tried it?

I can't take it. Minkulpa makes me sick. I tried it a couple of times but I got headaches and was vomiting. When you feel like that, you have to lie down with a moist cool towel over your eyes and wait till you feel better. It's not much fun! Your eyes feel like they are burning. Even if you are just helping to pick it you got to be careful not to rub your eyes. It burns like onions. You have to learn proper way with minkulpa. But many Anangu women really enjoy it. They go mad for minkulpa. It's a serious trade out here. Before the days of minkul people used to chew 'niggy niggy', a block of black tobacco given out with the rations. We were all looking like Clint Eastwood.

The minkulpa that grows in the hills is the strongest. Minkulpa that grows in the sand is not so strong. You can decide, but most kungkas prefer the stronger tobacco. Even when it is picked, you can tell the strength of it by its smell. Of course if it has a strong smell it is more potent to chew.

Spring is the best harvest. Minkulpa grows everywhere in the Anangu Lands at that time. It has a white flower and broad green leaves. It is not a really tall plant but stands by itself. Often minkulpa grows in clumps, for easier picking. Certain places are known for their regular and abundant crops. These places are often called minkul farms; it's an affectionate term. When the farms are ready to harvest we might pick enough to fill one blanket each, or more. Mostly we share the minkul but some people are greedier than others.

It is dried out in the sun. Often we lay the blanket full of minkul on an old bed base, and spread it out even. We have to train the dogs to stay off, even the children. It dries out fairly quickly, usually about eight hours. But when the sky is cloudy it might take two days. It changes colour when it is drying, from fresh green to a dusky green. Then we chop it up like tea leaf, and keep it in sealed containers or old milk tins. I hide mine for safekeeping.

You don't feel like having water when you chew minkulpa. You make your own moisture in your mouth. But you got to mix it with the ashes. You have to collect the ashes from the base of the gum tree. Look, same like this one. You mix it half and half, good mix. Put some ashes in the palm of your hand, then add dried minkulpa leaves and mix it together with your fingers. Sometimes you might spit on it to make a 'ball', some others just throw it in their mouths. It tastes a little bitter and when you take it from your mouth and put it down, it leaves a brown stain.

There's a funny story about minkulpa. Years ago some kungkas went to Cairns for a meeting I think. After a few days the motel manager asked if the kungkas knew how to use toilet paper. They didn't know what to say to that silly man. He told them his staff found brown marks on the sheets. Everyone laughed, and then he put saucers next to their beds, for their minkul.

Mavis Wari
My Story

In 1966 I went from Titjikala to the Barossa Valley for work. Before, I was working at Maryvale Station, then the Lutheran missionaries came to tell us to go to the Barossa Valley to pick some grapes. Pastor Albrecht used to drive his truck out from the Mission Block in Alice Springs to Titjikala, with fruit and clothing for us. He would give us church at Titjikala; he was the main missionary. So he drove me down south in his Holden car. The road between Alice Springs and Adelaide was a dirt road then, no bitumen. I only had a little case with my few belongings. I was sixteen years of age.

I worked for Mr and Mrs Paul Stiller at Bethany. They had a big stone house with a large veranda, at the base of Menglers Hill. My room was a sleepout on the front. It had an amazing view looking right over the Barossa Valley. Doris Thomas from Titjikala had stayed there before me. Her name was on the wall.

Helen Fly from Hermannsburg was there too. She stayed in the next house with Wally and Jean Stiller. The houses were on the same farm and Wally was Paul's son. They managed the farm together, and were a strict Lutheran family. Helen and I went with them each Sunday to their church in Tanunda. We got dressed up real nice, with white gloves and socks, and a pretty dress. We learnt all the hymns in English, but today I sing the hymns in Arrernte.

Helen and I worked out in the vineyards with Mr Stiller and his son. When the grapes were full and ready for picking, then it was really hard work.

I worked for Mrs Stiller too. Her name was Maria and she taught me domestic work. I would milk the cows by hand, in the old barn situated between the two houses. She taught me how to wash the clothes and bedsheets, using the scrubbing board and the old copper, where we boiled the linen till it was clean. The clothesline was a wire tied between two posts, near the laundry shed. There was a large flower garden and fruit trees close by.

My other work was to set the table properly for the meals, wash the dishes, and make the beds really nice each day. I also had to collect the eggs from the chicken house, count the eggs and put them in the boxes. Mrs Stiller used to sell the eggs. She also made jams to sell. We used to cut up the apricots and plums in the evenings. I used to go with her to sell the jam in Tanunda. She also sold dried fruit and sultanas. I helped to pack it in the bags for sale. There was always a lot of food because they grew it on the farm. They didn't stop.

Sometimes we visited their daughters' farms near Blyth. They would always share the fruits and vegetables, and their daughters' husbands would give them meat. I was surprised to see half-caste Aboriginal baby children there, because the Stillers were all German. They had adopted these kids. I didn't know where they came from, or what would happen to them, so I looked after them too. I grew to love them kids because I was missing all the family kids back home. Their names were Christopher and Ali(son).

At Christmas time I would travel back home to see my family. Issy Simpadober from the Lutheran Welfare would keep me company on the long trip back to Alice Springs. She was in charge of looking after all the kids that went to the Mission Block in Alice Springs. Sometimes we travelled by road, but I also flew on the Qantas aeroplane. I would go and visit my parents, and then travel back to the Barossa Valley for more work. Then Alison Wilyuka from Titjikala came down too. My niece Jennifer Summerfield came down to that place after me. She told me she used to look after Christopher and Ali too.

My last trip back home from there was by train, by myself. There were other Anangu people on the train travelling through Maree, Oodnadatta, Finke and Rodinga to Alice Springs. I came back to Titjikala to work in the school. It was a caravan school then; the vans were called 'silver bullets'. I used to clean them after school hours and wash the towels for the children.

Not long after I got back home there was a big rain. After the big rain there was a flood because someone had built a dam and it blocked the water and made the flood. The caravan school got broken in the flood, and the new permanent school building at Titjikala was built then. Even the train line got washed away. That's how the new train line was made, on the other side. No more train through Rodinga or Finke, because of that flood.

My wages from my time at the Barossa Valley had been sent to the Lutheran Trust at the Mission Block. So I had earnt a lot of money for my hard work. My brother-in-law Paulus Wilyuka taught me to drive a car so I bought a Holden car and used to drive everywhere to visit my families, even as far as Pipalyatjara, near the Western Australia border. It was all dirt roads back in those days. That Holden was a good strong car and I had learnt to drive well. Sometimes if we had to drive across a sandy creek I would let all the air out of the tyres so we could cross to the other side. Today we are spoilt with modern roads and four-wheel drives.

I worked for the health mob. It was a good job because I could drive so I could help him take all the people to Alice Springs for appointments and bring them back in the afternoon. Then I began to look after all the kids, when parents began going for drink (alcohol). We looked after lots of kids, me and my sister, who has passed away.

Sue Haseldine
Cleaning the Rockholes

I respect my culture and want to pass it on to my kids and grandkids. We go out to keep the rockholes clean, sometimes visiting sites too. It's about looking after the animals. It's about looking after the land. I try to protect the land at all costs. Without the land, you lose your soul. Without your soul, well, it's a big mental health issue. That's why I don't believe in any kind of mining. That will devastate our culture, any aspect of it.

Our country, that's our pharmacy. It's where our medicines come from. It is our grocery shop for food, our butcher shop for kuka (meat), our church for our spiritual needs. It is also our school, our education. Today we also respect two-way education, bush way plus mainstream.

It takes weeks to prepare trips to go out to clean the rockholes. Preparation includes who will travel, which cars, how much food and water and every necessary equipment. We travel with fresh food and tin food, and also gather bush tucker in season. We might catch wombat and kangaroo, cook them in the ashes.

We do these trips twice a year. One trip in September after the last of the rains, to keep the waterholes clean for summer. And then again in March or April in autumn, after summer.

It's rough work pulling camels, dingoes, emus and other birds out of rockholes. Sometimes we can use a pump. Mostly we use a bucket tied on a rope to the towbar, filling the buckets with bones and fur. It's dirty work getting covered in decaying bodies and shit. Sometimes the rockholes are so polluted birds won't even drink from it; sometimes not even ants! Only got the bush shower at the end of the day to wash off the shit. As much as we can, we clean the rockholes for the animals, for their sanctuary.

I try to cap the trips at twenty people. Sometimes if it's just family, it might only be ten people. Overseas people come with us; some donate to our cause. German, Lithuanian, Polish, Israelis, American, they all come for a cultural experience. We take these people out with us so they can appreciate our culture. So we can teach them our ways. They never forget; something moves them. Often they come back.

We ask for a contribution of $200 each, for food and fuel. That is how we fund the trips. Sometimes we take some help from government departments, but only the dollars without bribes. We collect and sell bottles and cans, fundraise any old way. Our greenie friends, they might run a sausage sizzle. It's just what we need to do.

An American congressman and his wife came to visit us once. Then the Wilderness Society heard about our work; turned it international. A documentary was made called *The Keeper*. It's been translated into Spanish and French. It's also been shown on New Zealand Maori television. So more people know about our work now. And how important my culture is to me.

Kaya Kaya Kelly (age ten years)
The Fish and the Man

The fish's name was Ian and the man's name was Seth. The man loved fishing.

So the man went fishing one day. Then he was hearing something. It was a fish singing. The fish was singing 'Don't worry, be happy' because the man wasn't catching any fish. The singing made the man feel happy.

After a while he was hearing something else. It was another song. The fish was singing 'Take me to the river, chuck me in the water' and the man started to laugh. He got happier.

When the man Seth caught the fish, the fish asked him, 'Can you please put me back in the water? I want to stay with my family'. The man said 'Yes, I will put you back in the water'. And he did. They became good friends. And the man visited the fish every day and every night.

Together they sang the song 'Here's a little song I wrote, you might want to sing it note by note, don't worry be happy'. And sometimes they did a little dance too. They were happy and promised to be friends forever. But Seth found a girlfriend.

Ian the fish waited all day and night, waiting for Seth to come and feed him, and sing the song with him. One day Ian saw Seth and his girlfriend walking along the beach looking happy, and he started to cry.

Ian started singing out, 'Seth, Seth'. He sang out, 'Come and feed me, I'm hungry'. He waited for a long time. But when Seth did come, the fish was gone. Seth sang out, 'Ian, Ian, I'm sorry what I did forgetting you. I'll never do that again. You are my friend'.

The fish came back. The fish said, 'I thought you was my real friend, Seth'. And Seth said, 'I'm sorry Ian, can you forgive me?'

At night time, if you listen, you can hear them singing the song again, 'Don't worry, be happy'.

* The songs referenced are 'Don't Worry Be Happy' by Bobby McFerrin (1988) and 'Take Me to the River' by Al Green (1974).

Rosie Lester

Walatina poem

You got no shame
    that's not your ngura
    that's not your land
    that's not your wapar
You got no claim
You got no right

    my katja's ngura
    my tjamus too
    my mama tjuta
    my children's ngura
It's not for you
To do as you please

They nuked it out
Poisoned the land
Took life away
For their own selfish
Reign
    you got no shame

They drilled for oil
They think it's theirs
Cracked the ground
    still no shame

You let them in
This is your sins
You hurt us mob
You just don't care

Where is your spirit
Do the right thing!
Get back to your country

You got no respect
You forgot what is right
You let that dollar
Control your choice

Money don't cry for you
When you're dead and gone

The country never forgets
The Spirit is strong
It is watching you
Everything you do wrong

Ngura: camp/home   Wapar: story (might be Dreamtime story)
Katja: son   Tjamus: grandfathers

Lionel G Fogarty
small trees sea inland mobs

Small trees sea inland mobs
The Yalata man leaf over from old mission,
Sun cold afternoon session.
Yalata womens all sort of speak in sign too.
Peace walks the no grog town,
No school no pool swinging
Store price as high as money taken by the needed.
Houses are big. Filled with small things in wanting
    more.
If you are family be careful of your pocket.
Age care wants art taken to young care.
Lot of cars, many feet move slow, worker on the rubbish
    around cleans
When big note shots come to town.
Yalata big times shopping is 4 houses away
Ya better understand some lingo for lazy yarns are you to
    get play full
For word over minds
Two groups of languages all know each other's.
Not hot in autumn but cold in winter.
Yalata man we like ya

Yalata woman we need your happy smile eyes and speak
   low as the desert,
Makes my life your lights.
Meeting with Yalata man's was a happy to meet, say
   where you're from, same place been there in meeting,
   you're dead ok
They know there places as the beaches lay the water
   don't stay
Shine down the nose off a wombat gives times to hunt
   slow and fast for old young turkeys too.
My story is travelling there and here, life happen on, was
   to go to and when to come back.
Trip to the land is a shop not far,
Meeting are arrangement in wait of languages
Some people have stories but in bit and wave like waters
   in freed to seas
Movement on to get some thing seen fast
Humbugged happen was cuss on cuss until every one
   found.
He drank with in that park but now hometown is they
   are.
People taken story not return
Some not wanting to tell
Driving car and work for Malu trail
Family life has to be talked
New gestation as new housing
I am out, the dogs are about, men walk with the dogs of
   every kind
Yet no vegetable plants, many water tanks for the people
   are in needs.

Yalata man be free, Yalata women be free, we think of
your days.

Lionel G. Fogarty is a Murri poet and political activist. The first of his many books
was published in 1980.

CPSIA information can be obtained at www.ICGtesting.com
Printed in the USA
LVOW11s1617170316

479627LV00002B/16/P

9 781742 586212